LIVING'S THE S

CARMEN MARTÍN GAITE (1925–2000) was one of Spain's most distinguished novelists. Born in Salamanca, she published her first novel at the age of 29 and won the Premio Gijón. Her subsequent novels won many awards. The publication of *Variable Cloud* was a considerable event in Spain, where it topped the bestseller lists for several weeks. *The Farewell Angel* won the Spanish National Prize for Literature.

ANNE MCLEAN has translated Latin American and Spanish novels, short stories, memoirs and other writings by authors including Julio Cortázar, Orlando González Esteva, Ignacio Padilla, Luis Sepúlveda, Paula Varsavsky and Javier Cercas.

By the same author in English translation

VARIABLE CLOUD

THE FAREWELL ANGEL

Carmen Martín Gaite

LIVING'S THE STRANGE THING

Translated from the Spanish
by Anne McLean

THE HARVILL PRESS
LONDON

Published by The Harvill Press, 2004
2 4 6 8 10 9 7 5 3 1

Originally published with the title *Lo raro es vivir* by Anagrama, Barcelona, 1996

This edition has been translated with the financial assistance of the Spanish Dirección General del Libro y Bibliotecas, Ministerio de Cultura

First published in Great Britain in 2004 by
The Harvill Press
Random House, 20 Vauxhall Bridge Road,
London SW1V 2SA

Random House Australia (Pty) Limited
20 Alfred Street, Milsons Point, Sydney,
New South Wales 2061, Australia

Random House New Zealand Limited
18 Poland Road, Glenfield,
Auckland 10, New Zealand

Random House South Africa (Pty) Limited
Endulini, 5A Jubilee Road, Parktown 2193, South Africa

The Random House Group Limited Reg. No. 954009
www.randomhouse.co.uk/harvill

A CIP catalogue record for this book
is available from the British Library

ISBN 1 84343 037 1

Papers used by Random House are natural, recyclable products made from wood grown in sustainable forests; the manufacturing processes conform to the environmental regulations of the country of origin

Typeset in Fournier by Palimpsest Book Production Limited
Printed and bound in Great Britain by
Mackays of Chatham plc, Chatham, Kent

Contents

For Lucila Valente,
always turning up
amid ruins and blunders
smiling light itself

No-one can step twice into the same
river, nor touch mortal substance twice
in the same condition. By the speed of its
change it scatters and gathers again.

– Heraclitus of Ephesus

I

The Crystal Planet

There are times when, in the blink of an eye, normality turns extraordinary and we become aware of it without quite knowing how. From among the countless expressions, movements and inklings that swell the shapeless mass of daily life, one, apparently insignificant, splits off from the rest and jumps like a discordant note off a stave, resonating in the air like the buzzing of a bluebottle – what's going on, is this a breakdown or the beginning of something new, we look at our hands, our knees, what's changed, where to focus, I don't know. And then comes fear or paralysis.

This was the kind of scare that crept up behind me two years ago, on the 30th of June, when I'd just parked in a providential spot beneath that shabby split-cane roof, around seven in the evening. I'd executed the manoeuvre impeccably, though I am usually so clumsy when it comes to things like that and always think it a miracle when I don't bang into something or a policeman doesn't show up. I'd spent the drive listening to a Sade tape, those heartrending laments in English always anaesthetise me, freeing the gaze, shifting clouds, warm breeze, not much traffic; and suddenly I was tense and frightened, unable to take the key out of the ignition, I've been fooling myself, everything's going wrong, from now on you'd better watch yourself.

I walked carefully across the gravel towards the unfamiliar building, relieved that no-one was following me. There was a somewhat squalid garden with boxwood borders, wooden benches in need of a coat of paint, and a fountain with a frog staring at the sky and spouting a little stream from his mouth. The wind had picked up quite a bit. The outline of the mountains was visible in the distance, and some big leaden clouds, perforated by pinpricks of light, were gathering near the Valle de los Caídos.

I went up some steps and stopped before going in. A few windows were open, but I could hear no sounds nor see any shapes moving about inside. On the door I found the plaque that convinced me I was at the right place, capital letters in green and blue tiles, and underneath, also in tiles, protected by a little roof, a normal-sized Our Lady of Perpetual Help in her hieratic, iconic pose, neutral eyes, unenthusiastically holding the child who looks like an asparagus spear with his tilted head, both of them underfed, she in her calotte; almost all the virgins in the world clutch their babies' fingers as if duty-bound and betray themselves with an apprehensive smile: I wonder what I've got coming; after they paint this portrait and take down the decorative angels, I'll have maternity and mythology to put up with.

I shuddered as I went in. On the left, behind a glass counter, was a middle-aged woman in a white lab coat, her hair pulled tightly back in a bun. The light filtering through the gauze curtains was also white, as were the floor and the walls and the chairs and a smell that was also white and tenuous, like rosemary spirit. The woman was on the phone and, seeing me standing there, motioned with her chin for me to step aside and wait. I moved back a little and stood watching silhouettes moving behind a door of frosted glass that was slightly ajar. There must have been a garden on the other side, because I could see oscillating shadows of leaves and branches crowning the heads of those figures, coming together and moving apart erratically, as if swaying in the wind to an uneven rhythm. Their hushed voices reached me as well, and when they appeared in the gap in the door I could focus on them fleetingly, and see they were wearing dark clothing. One of them stopped and leaned in to look at me with smiling, bulging eyes, waved and skipped away. She was a woman, but wore a priest's cassock.

After a while the other woman, the one in the white lab coat, who'd now finished her telephone conversation, rang something that looked like a bicycle bell on a metal stand, and I realised she was calling me. I went over.

"I'm here for Room 309," I said. "To visit Don Basilio Luengo."

She blinked nervously. "You'll have to speak to the director first. He asked me to notify him of your arrival. He was expecting you this morning."

"I couldn't make it."

She stood up without taking her eyes off me, came out of her glassed-in station and walked ahead of me down a red-and-white-tiled corridor to a stained-glass door with ornate ironwork. She opened it, turned on the lights with a switch on the right and stepped aside to let me enter. "Wait in the lounge. He'll be here in a moment. If you get bored, there's the *Encyclopaedia Espasa* to look at."

Aside from the *Espasa*, carefully arranged in an enormous mahogany bookshelf that took up half the wall, the room's furnishings consisted of two sets of antique armchairs, a grandfather clock and an abundance of little games tables, covered in green baize and scattered about. On the right, half-covered by a worn damask curtain, was a platform reached by three wooden steps. I heard noises behind the curtain and walked towards it. A man in blue overalls was crouched down fitting a socket. There were pliers and lengths of wire on the floor. I stood watching him work. After a short time he collected his tools, lifted a large white jug that was leaning against the skirting board and took a long drink. Then he turned off the light, came down the steps and crossed the room. The peak of his cloth cap was turned to the back.

"If there's nothing else you people need done," he said, stopping for a moment when he caught sight of me.

"No. Nothing for me," I answered, after an imperceptible hesitation.

"Well, I'll say goodbye then. That wire was completely burnt out. You could have had a short circuit."

He pointed to the portrait of an ancient bearded gentleman presiding over the room with medals on his chest, and to the gilded brass wall lamp topping it off like a cornice.

"I'll fix your man's light another time," he said, "I'm running late today."

He headed for the door I'd come through and disappeared without another word.

The wait dragged on, seeming all the longer because the shutters were tightly closed against the lingering daylight outside. The room smelled a bit damp, though I couldn't see any leaks. What light there was came from some alabaster wall lamps that shone up towards the ceiling. I remained standing, transfixed by a combination of anxiety and alarm. I lit a cigarette, but stubbed it out straight away because it made me feel sick.

On the *Espasa* bookshelf, the *España* volume was missing. As I was noticing this and beginning to suspect it might be found in Room 309, I sensed a presence behind me and turned round with a start. There was a brief but intense silence.

"Sorry to have kept you waiting," said the man, offering me his long, youthful hand, and shaking mine firmly. "Welcome."

It was the same voice I'd heard over the phone, but now it was much more persuasive because it so perfectly fitted the manner and face of its owner. I was surprised to find myself wondering anxiously what kind of impression I was making, a forgotten, adolescent curiosity I'd felt around older men to whom I was attracted at first sight, and who made me feel insecure. I suddenly remembered with dismay how I was dressed and the mess my hair was in and wished I'd had a shower and put on some deodorant. The man was tall, wearing a dark grey linen suit and white shirt without a tie. He didn't look as young as I'd thought he was at first, though his hands and voice certainly were. I guessed he was about 50, one of those people who smile without actually smiling, a nice body, a few grey hairs. We were looking directly at one another and I didn't say a thing.

"Shall we sit down?" he asked.

We sat facing each other on antique chairs with black wooden armrests and yellow upholstery and cushions. I still hadn't said a word, and I was no longer able to meet his gaze. I could still feel him staring at me and my heart was pounding in my chest.

"I can't get over how much you look like your mother," he said. "I suppose you've been hearing that forever."

"People have told me that, yes. Although, lately . . . well, for years now . . . my friends and hers haven't really moved in the same circles, so . . . well, there weren't many opportunities to compare us."

"Do you mean you had no contact with your mother?"

"Let's call it a distant relationship."

"Well," he said in a serious tone, "I'd nonetheless like to offer my condolences for the loss, whatever its extent, that her death must have caused you. She was an extraordinary woman."

"Thank you. I know."

"And she loved you very much."

"Now *that* I don't know. But it doesn't matter," I added, looking back up at the tall man with a sudden toughness intended to thwart any assertion he might make to the contrary. "I haven't come here to discuss that, as I'm sure you'll understand."

I immediately regretted my scowl, which I saw reflected in his gentle, ironic, perhaps even slightly compassionate gaze as in a distorting mirror. It's an expression that puts years on me.

"So you already know what you've come here to discuss, do you?"

I felt I was losing ground, but I kept my guard up.

"No, I haven't the faintest idea. Remember, it was you who summoned me here and wanted to talk to me."

"And does it bother you that we're talking?"

"No. Look, I'm sorry I spoke to you like that. It's just that I'm feeling a bit defensive. I suppose it would do me good to talk to someone. And the less familiar the better."

"Well then, just relax and carry on with whatever occurs to you. In your grandfather's opinion, people who write the contents page before they write the book never get to the bottom of things. I sometimes ask him if he's written any books himself, but he says no, or at least not that he recalls, memory's a tricky thing, he says. Of course, I think he's the tricky one."

He smiled at me and I timidly smiled back. He knew a lot, this tall man. He scared me a little. The grandfather clock struck a quarter to eight.

"I'm sorry," I said, "would you mind opening the shutters? I find the light in here rather oppressive."

He hesitated.

"Ah, there's a slight problem. The windows open on to the back garden and they're all out there at the moment, it's their recreation time before supper. This room fascinates them. If they notice the shutters open even the tiniest bit, they crowd round to peer in, and goodbye privacy. I don't imagine you'd like that."

"God no, how horrible, that's the last thing I need."

"Well, I need it even less. Don't forget I spend all day looking after them. However," he added, "we could improve things a bit. Those lights belong in a funeral parlour."

He dragged a floor lamp over and plugged it in nearby. It gave off a strong, slightly bluish light. Then he went over to the door and turned off the other lights.

"That's better, isn't it?" he asked, sitting down again and crossing his legs. "More intimate."

"Yes, much better. Thank you. By the way, is my grandfather in the garden?"

"No, he hardly ever leaves his room, except very late at night to talk to the stars. He lives a life apart. He's a special case."

There was a silence that seemed to last too long. I didn't know how to break it. "Well, if you say so" was a handy phrase, but so banal that I dismissed it before it could escape from my mouth in a comic-strip speech bubble. I straightened up from my indolent slouch. Better to try another tack.

"Does my grandfather know I've come to see him?" I asked. "Or haven't you told him yet?"

"No. That's precisely what I wanted to talk to you about. I haven't told him, nor am I going to. He thinks she's the one who should come. It's her he's been waiting for."

The room began to spin towards an unknown orbit. Or rather, approaching in a spin was another planet that was about to crash into ours. And Mum arrived seated within that planet, which had crystal walls so you could see what was happening inside. Not that anything really surprising was going on, it was a replica of the scene the tall man and I were enacting at that moment, with one difference: sheltered by those transparent walls, he was talking to Mum, not me. He leaned towards her and offered her a white handkerchief to dry her eyes, from which flowed crystal tears like those that bathe the faces of images of Our Lady of Sorrows. The room was decorated exactly the same, even the blue light that swept it like a lighthouse beam mirrored the rays from the floor lamp he'd recently turned on to provide intimacy; Mum's shoulders were trembling. What were they saying? I couldn't quite hear them over the strident buzzing of that oblong planet flying over our heads like a zeppelin tracing ever more dizzying spirals, so low, so close that I was gripped by panic. We were going to disintegrate in that unknown space before he'd even had time to tell me the story. There was no way out. Everything was spinning.

I covered my ears, squeezed my eyes shut and bent forwards, seeking the shelter of another body to accompany my trembling with its own.

"What's the matter? Are you feeling ill?"

"Ill, yes, very ill . . ."

I slipped on to the carpet, felt his hands on my hair and fainted.

Then, it must have been almost immediately, we were sitting side by side on the yellow sofa and he was taking my pulse. The expression on his face, though worried, communicated safety and gentleness rather than alarm. Strangely enough, I remembered everything, I didn't need to ask "Where am I?", "What happened?" or "Who are you?" I simply surrendered to the pleasure of feeling protected while making sure I could no longer hear the vibrations of the crystal planet that had been about to crash into ours.

"Have you had anything to drink this evening or taken any drugs?" he asked, his eyes glued to his wristwatch.

"No."

"Lean your head back, would you? Breathe deeply, slow down. That's it, that's better."

I left my hand lying gently on my striped skirt, I don't know why I'd worn such an ugly thing. As he took his fingers away, he brushed mine briefly, perhaps professionally. Or not?

"That was a very strange blackout," he said. "And so sudden! You're not pregnant, are you?"

"Me, pregnant?" I objected. "God forbid. I never, ever want to have children. Not in a million years."

"Well then, you'd better be careful because you're very beautiful. And please, don't be upset."

He handed me a white handkerchief, and that was when I realised I was crying.

I was grateful he didn't ask me any questions. I even began to suspect, as I was drying my eyes, that if I told him about the planet, instead of proceeding to explore my possible Oedipal complex, he'd have said: "If you think you saw it, that's what happened. We don't all see the same things." That suspicion, or rather fantasy, gave me the strength to stand up and walk across the room to the platform where I'd seen the man in blue overalls. I was very thirsty and remembered the jug must still be there. The action of lifting it with my tensed, slightly bent arms, and letting a cool stream of water fall towards my mouth, confirmed the flexibility of my body, quenched my thirst, and sent clear ideas and a zest for life shooting up to my mind. The jug also confirmed that the electrician hadn't been a figment of my imagination. Why then would the image of my mother crying crystal tears have been one? I had seen both in the same room. A few drops spilt down my front and I dried them with the tall man's handkerchief, which I still had in the pocket of my jacket. Then I slowly retraced my steps, delighting in their rhythm. The tall man had called me beautiful. And now he'd be watching the way I moved.

"I'm sure there's going to be a storm," I said, when I sat back down beside him. "Thanks for the handkerchief."

He glanced briefly at it as he took it. I don't wear mascara or make-up. It wasn't stained. He folded it.

"Do you want to keep talking about your grandfather?" he asked after a short pause. "Or do you want to leave it for now?"

"I'd rather continue. Why did you say before that he's waiting for her? Doesn't he know she died? It's been eight weeks."

He looked at me seriously.

"Precisely. And during those eight weeks his closest relative, who I believe would be yourself, has neither telephoned nor perhaps would have shown up at all if I had not thought to phone her. Or am I mistaken?"

"No, you're not mistaken."

"So what do you expect? You think I should have told him? I just kept the newspapers out of his reach during the couple of days when there were articles about her. Although I don't really know if that did any good."

"Do you mean he still might have seen one?"

"Maybe, although he's not generally interested in newspapers. He prefers the *Espasa*. He says it's the funniest thing on earth."

I looked towards the space the *España* volume had left on the shelf. Now I was sure he had it. And all the changes our country had undergone since the publication of that encyclopaedia hit me in a jarring whirlwind. How would my grandfather have experienced those changes, especially those of the last few years, including – wavering, feckless and clumsy – my own growing up?

"Has he said anything about me?" I asked.

"No. Not about her either. That's the strange thing. He doesn't ask after her, doesn't even mention her name. Before, if she wasn't away on a trip – in which case she sent him postcards – she came to see him once or twice a month, although never on a fixed day, which he found thrilling. Those visits lasted well into the evening, nothing like the ones other people pay their aged parents. You could tell that for them this was no distressing obligation, but rather a pleasure, something they enjoyed. I read these things in people's faces even when they aren't obvious, but your mother and grandfather made it easy for me. It was especially obvious that he lived for those visits, revelling in the anticipation and the memories. 'My daughter's coming today,

I'm sure of it,' he'd tell me one morning, out of the blue. And he was usually right. He hasn't said it since. And he talks to me less. He hasn't telephoned her to see if anything's wrong either, I've asked Reception to let me know if he does. They had a sort of pact, she once told me, not to bother each other by phone, except in an emergency."

"Sounds just like Mum," I said, as if to myself. "But what intrigues me is how my grandfather could have found out. Do you know Rosario Tena? Does the name mean anything to you?"

He gestured ambiguously.

"She shared my mother's studio for the last few years," I explained, not taking my eyes off him.

"Sure. But she hasn't been here."

"She might have written."

"No, I assure you."

"Then, I don't know, let me think . . ."

He shrugged his shoulders.

"Best not to think about it. Guessing how Don Basilio learns things is as difficult as knowing what he finds out and what he doesn't. But what difference does it make? All that matters is the alchemy with which he transforms the amorphous information that reaches him. His obstinacy in making hallucinations a way of life is unshakeable and redemptive. It's what allows him to carry on. And I can assure you," he continued solemnly, as if pronouncing a verdict, "that he'll keep waiting for her until she shows up."

Now he was looking at me with his left eyebrow slightly raised. It was a gesture of complicity, a plea for acquiescence. I knew he was seeing her, talking to her, just as he'd been doing inside the crystal planet. He was starting to think she was back. I wrenched my eyes away.

"You want me to impersonate her?" I asked.

"I'd simply like to know whether you're prepared to collaborate with me. It depends on your courage and your capacity for dangerous games. It's up to you to make a move or leave the table."

A wave of heat rose from my feet, engulfing me and bringing me back to myself. Dry leaves and archival papers burned up in that bonfire.

"It's been a long time since I've played at anything. What should I do?" I asked. "You'll need to bring me up-to-date."

"Of course. And you me. We hardly know each other. But, for a start, it would be in our interest to trust each other, at least a little bit."

I held out my hand. "You can take that as given as far as I'm concerned."

"Don't rush things. It'll take time," he replied, not letting go of the hand he was grasping in his. "And it'll impose its own conditions, don't you think? But this is an encouraging way to begin. By the way, you're even prettier when you smile."

"I'll keep it in mind. Anything else?"

"Yes, of course, much more."

I didn't see my grandfather that 30th of June. By the time we noticed, it was too late, and the tall man said that the rules of the game were now set, and in any case it would be better to have a break, and to do things comfortably. Wait for the right moment. He wasn't more specific than that. I understood that we were playing already.

"Let me kiss your hand," he said as we were saying goodbye in the front hall. "Your mother liked it."

It was dark by then and there were big clouds overhead. I crossed the gravel without turning round and when I started the engine he was gone. Right before I reached Madrid, by the Cuesta de las Perdices, the storm broke. Just as Sade was singing:

"There's a quiet storm
and I've never felt this hot before . . ."

I wound down the car windows to let in the smell of wet earth.

II

First Lies

The urgent need to continue that story threads the days that followed together in my memory, though I certainly didn't expect to be the one guiding the needle to sew it all up. But the knots inside forced me to contemplate the welter of decisions which, in spite of myself, kept springing up only to dissolve in a flutter of fallen petals as soon as they appeared. In similarly knotty times, I have often failed to recognise that they'd untangled themselves without any effort on my part. Experience doesn't carry over to the next time, on the contrary, it buries its head in the sand. A few days later, suddenly aware that the waters had subsided, I remember saying "That should have been so easy!" and cursing my blindness, but when the same thing happens again, weaving its tendrils around some other matter, I still imagine that turning it over and over in my mind might be of some use.

Furthermore, the question of my grandfather affected lots of other matters, and I'd wanted to ignore that. I thought – whether mistakenly or not – that getting in the car to go and visit him on that 30th of June was a mere formality, free of danger. The next morning it was already impossible to ignore the residual flood spreading across landscapes more difficult to describe or survey. The underwater pipes had burst during the night in one of my dreams. Dad had appeared, very angry, demanding an explanation for the odours invading his new suburban home; his little boy had woken up saying "poo-poo!"; eventually they found a big hole in the ground beside the pool, and soon Dad, though he was not known for his perspicacity, had guessed that the gushing filth mucking up their lawn was overflowing from my cesspool. "Do you deny it?" "Of course not," I told him. He was gesturing extravagantly, wearing tinted sunglasses with fluorescent frames and demanding, as he pointed at his mud-caked trousers, that my husband send one of his workers over as soon as possible; he refers to Tomás as "your husband" even though he knows he isn't.

I had other dreams about pipes and tangled wires, but I didn't remember them so clearly. I only know that in one of them the man in the blue overalls was there, saying: "You people were just about to have a short circuit." At his feet a kind of snarled intestine stirred.

I woke up early with a terrible headache and couldn't get back to sleep, although my alarm clock hadn't yet gone off. As I was pouring my coffee and getting my toast ready, Tomás rang from Jaén, where they were working on a housing development. He remarked that my voice sounded a bit strange.

"Haven't woken you up, have I, gorgeous?"

"No," I said. "My father woke me up with some nuisance and put me in a bad mood. He's got a problem with a sewage pipe. He wants you to go and have a look at it – as if you didn't have anything better to do."

"Go where?" Tomás asked, somewhat taken aback.

"His villa in Las Rozas."

"He has a villa in Las Rozas? First I've heard of it."

"Yeah. He told us the day of Mum's funeral. In a subdivision near there. They moved a little while ago, they're giving up the flat in Madrid, moving up in the world. You know, boredom makes people complicate their lives and Montse gets bored. Dad wants me to go and see them, he drew me a map, I told you, don't you remember?"

"No," he said, "but it doesn't matter. Though it does seem

odd that your father phoned to ask me a favour, when we hardly know each other."

"Well, there you go."

"I suppose you told him I'm away."

"No. I didn't tell him anything. Maybe he'll forget. He's like that."

There was a silence that suddenly became heavy. I took a sip of my coffee and glanced at the clock.

"And what about you, how are you?" he asked.

"Me? Fine."

"You sure?"

"Of course. Why?"

"I don't know, your voice doesn't sound right. I'd give anything to be able to see you right now."

"You'd regret it. I'm ugly."

"Impossible."

"I'm telling you, worse than ugly, mutant. I'm wearing a brown dress like a nun's habit, made out of lilac-and-gold embossed cloth, my hair's dyed platinum blonde, and I've got varicose veins. Oh, I almost forgot, I had a nose job too; but to make it bigger, you know, not smaller."

While I was coming out with that pack of nonsense I imagined a parallel scene in a movie, in which a woman, without letting go of the telephone, moves so she can be caressed by her lover. She motions to him to be careful. It's a scene I've watched many times though I've never done it myself. In that erotic fantasy, my lover's hands were those of the tall man.

Tomás started to laugh.

"Come on, don't be such a brat. Did you go and see your grandfather?"

"Yes."

"And how did it go?"

"He was asleep. I'll have to go back. He seems to have accepted my mother's death quite well. That's all I was worried about, you know. When are you coming home?"

"I think I'm going to be another week. What you should do is ask for leave and forget about grandfathers and fathers and family. After all, for the amount of attention they pay you . . ."

The tall man began to unbutton my pyjamas. He did it slowly, without taking his eyes off me. I grabbed his hand with my left one, turned it upwards and began to kiss first the palm, then each of the fingers. He offered no resistance. The fact that I didn't know his name somewhat hindered my fantasy.

"You need a rest and it's beautiful here," Tomás said. "Why don't you come down? There's an inn up in the Sierra de Cazorla, a few kilometres from here, with unbelievable views, away from everything, no noise, a real Eden."

"Thanks, but you know how I feel about Edens. Besides, they gave me a week off when Mum died and I don't want to take my holiday until August. Work's what keeps me focused."

"Suit yourself, as long as you're all right."

"I'm fine, I told you. Hey, sweetheart, seriously, I'm going to be late, my coffee's getting cold."

When I hung up the phone, I realised in amazement that I'd told Tomás two huge lies for no particular reason – that my father had rung and that my grandfather had been asleep – and barely even noticed as I was speaking that I was making them up. They weren't white lies or even defensive ones; they were fatal, the kind that sting treacherously like wasps. The sting starts to swell and smart and suddenly you feel like you've done something wrong. I sensed that those two statements would have consequences, whether I admitted to having lied or not. Tomás is a persistent and fervent cultivator of logic, *madre mía*, a storm cloud of half-baked explanations approached, luckily he wouldn't be back for another week. A little red warning light went on in my head and pulsated for a while, but went out in the shower.

Anyway, I took note of the fact that my visit to my grandfather had exposed a number of wires from various sources that were about to cause a short circuit.

But I was wrong to believe that by immersing myself in my work – the one calming decision I made as I dried my hair – I would find a way out of that dense undergrowth.

III

Down to the Woods

When I travel by metro, I tend to think a lot, with lightning flashes, crackles of high voltage that generate rivers of unanswerable questions and run into their own ends, the gloomy stretches of that interior voyage accentuating the discontinuity between logic and terror. I've been aware of it, and frightened by it, since I was a little girl, but I liked it too; then, of course, the sensation of defencelessness at feeling myself alive among strangers was palliated by my unconditional connection to the woman who, besides being my link to the world, knew so much about subterranean voyages: my mother.

I called those trips by metro "going down to the woods", although I didn't know until later that this metaphor, like all metaphors, could conquer other territories. I didn't know what a metaphor was, but like all somewhat clever children, I invented lots of them.

Later, in my defiant teenage years, I'd descend into the metro like someone accepting a risky proposition, knowing that underground voyages are never innocent and always entangling. For the last ten years or so, I've avoided that method of urban locomotion, preferring to travel on the surface. People say the subway systems in big cities are dangerous these days, but that's not the reason. I avoid going down to the woods in general, to all the woods that proliferated gradually and imperceptibly from that first childhood metaphor.

"The muddle begins in people's legs; they're the trees, but

there's more to it," I said to myself on that first day of July, shortly after being dragged almost off my feet into the metro carriage and being shoved sharply as the doors closed. I was overwhelmed by how different people's legs are – from each other's and from mine – although apparently so similar, all supporting an unseen weight: the brain trying to keep itself alert, tired limbs, stomachs in breakfast-digesting trances, full lungs longing for a sigh; some bare, others wrapped in trousers or tights of different colours and textures, ending in shoes that grope blindly for space to plant themselves – feet and legs have their own gestures, not just when they're walking, but when they're leaning against a bar or a door, and especially when they shift from rest to movement. To classify legs by their gestures and thereby investigate the secret passageways of the soul would be an enormous task, requiring an entire team, of course, and moreover one would need to complement this objective evidence with testimony furnished by the next-of-kin – that is, those who would once have recognised without fail a certain one of those live columns by its gesture and still carry the impression etched on the back of their eyes, ready to reawaken at the slightest provocation, even though it might belong to a person who is dead or lost. Doesn't matter if we're on the 23rd floor of a building in Atlanta; if we look out the window and below us, among the swarming bustle of the avenue, someone crossing the street puts their right leg forward in that particular way, our heart leaps and then a name comes spontaneously to our lips. We might well ask ourselves what that person could have come to do in this city, or beat a retreat with the poisoned arrow of the hallucination stuck in our back – it can't be true, although you would have sworn it was, and we close our eyes remembering how the birds sang on the day of their funeral.

The relatives' testimony would be archived, naturally, in separate files; many unemployed sociologists could be given jobs, depending on the subsidies available – these days there doesn't seem to be much interest in this type of investigation, relating gestures to conduct suggests poking around in boggy terrain.

I was very surprised that my digressions weren't cut off by so much lurching, toe-stamping and elbowing, and that I was able to concentrate in such detail on the proportionate differences my neighbours in the carriage possessed from the waist down; at the same time I nurtured another question, intriguing enough by itself: Why had I taken the metro this morning, especially at rush hour?

When I'd come out of the house, the car had been parked right outside the door, an incredible bit of luck considering how the neighbourhood's getting, but I'd looked at it indifferently, walked on by and turned down the first street on the right, humming an old song of mine, "Living's the Strange Thing". I became engrossed by the thought that I considered it old, since the lyrics, the chords and the heartbreak that gave rise to it were still so fresh, having dripped not long before from the walls of a blue-papered garret, my first refuge after leaving my mother's house, how distant, how near, how strange, "living's the strange thing, rock of diamonds and spades, in-between-rock of living with severed sorrows, rock of survival . . ."; I walked without hurrying, though aware that I was running late and the entrance to the metro wasn't what you would call nearby; or rather, I wasn't really aware of anything. Until I found myself on the platform and let myself be swept by the avalanche of people that put me on one of the last carriages, I hadn't asked myself a single question, not even if this was the right line or whether I needed to change, it was the first time I'd gone to work by this means of transport.

"But in this case, as in so many, the means and ends can diverge or be joined by a fortuitous link," I continued to think as I changed position and tried to adjust my body to the others, like someone fitting pieces into a puzzle. "What's happened today is that I've simply felt tempted, without knowing why, to wander down to the woods, to sever ties with the predictable."

I'd started to make my way over to another platform, where it seemed a bit less crowded, and stopped in the corridor, took a deep breath like a tired swimmer and grabbed on to those five little words as to a life preserver: "go down to the woods". I wanted to remember when I'd first glimpsed their power as a metaphor, what had happened for me to understand it, "Something that propagates other things," my mother had said, "infects them; the woods can get inside you, or into a room, and you see trees where there aren't any," but where were we when she'd said it, and how did it come up in conversation? I tried to recapture my expression of childish surprise, it was probably summer, and someone else was there, maybe still my father? Forcing a memory to come out of hiding requires concentration and I didn't have it, it's like making your way through the dense undergrowth of the woods themselves, the mist filtering down, it's night, wolves might appear, but mysteries close themselves up in there, and anyone who's not going down to the woods can leave; you need to close your eyes. And perhaps pray.

I was pushed and fell into a seat someone had just left. I felt a tug on my handbag strap and turned in that direction. It was a very small boy in his mother's arms, she was distracted and her lips moved as she stared into space looking overwhelmed. The child interrogated me smilingly with his black, black eyes set in an ivory face; he'd completely entered my orbit. I, for my part, needed to pass my question on to him, as in one of those guessing games. I leaned over to his ear, and whispered "met-a-phor" and he began to wave his hands in delight, while writhing, imprisoned, on that familiar, hostile lap. The mother noticed nothing, unable to play, absorbed in her worries.

"Bippy!" the child said. And he stretched out his arms to me. It sounded like "pretty".

I couldn't help but think that he wanted to come with me. I stood up abruptly without looking back at him and nudged my way through the crowd like a miscreant, fleeing from the attempt at a wail I heard behind me. When I reached the door we were pulling out of a station and I just had time to read the sign which was already vanishing. "Next stop, change for Line Five," said the loudspeaker at the same moment. OK, get your head together, that station would be fine, I worked out that it wasn't too far from my destination. If I walked quickly, I could still make it almost on time.

Remembering where I was going pulled me halfway out of my lethargy. All those people knew where they were going, I'd almost lost my bearings, confused and cancelled out by movements extraneous to mine, almost suppressed the fragile nexus between the rhythm of swells and courses of ships – another metaphor, and a trivial one at that – I was anxious to get up to the surface, where houses are houses and streets are streets; I'd walk for a while along familiar streets and that would help clear my head.

I sighed, nevertheless, with a certain sense of nostalgia. Obeying that command was equal to murdering my embryonic riffs of thought, it was like prohibiting access to spermatozoa who rush to fertilise an egg or destroying them once they'd managed to get in – I'd always favoured the former, abortion terrified me. Enough, I didn't want to give wings to this latest metaphor, it was one of those that sting, I'd get off at the next stop, the end of the woods.

"Excuse me, are you getting off?" I asked a jacket lodged between mine and the door.

My cheek was buried in the shoulder pad. It was a somewhat worn drill jacket, impregnated with the smell of cigarette smoke. Its owner turned so I could see his profile, said yes with half a smile, and then said my name. He was wearing dark glasses and he was skinny. I knew him, obviously, but couldn't remember where from.

On the platform he greeted me warmly with a kiss and we started walking together towards the exit. His strides were long but loose, he was in no hurry.

"What a daze you're in, mate! You probably don't even remember who I am," he said.

"'Course I do, it's just that it's been so long since we've seen each other."

"Yeah, ages. But you're still daydreaming, I was watching you on the train and you were making me laugh, looked as though you were talking to yourself. You didn't even see me, obviously."

"You were watching me? Sorry, I didn't notice. Well, at this time of day we're all like zombies, don't you think? And then the metro gets so packed, we're lucky to escape unscathed."

I stole a few sidelong glances as we were talking, trying to place him among my old acquaintances. I began a mental review of certain bars I used to go to before I moved in with Tomás, to see whether, mixed in with some of those exotic names, the one belonging to this drill-jacketed guy would leap out, but it was such a labyrinthine trail that it threatened to turn into another wood, I've tramped around Madrid by the light of street lamps far too often. In any case he was a rhizomorph, no doubt about that. To avoid misunderstandings, we'd grouped the companions of my reckless youth under the generic name of rhizomorphs, a classification which allowed for subspecies, like botany. It was a metaphor Tomás had invented after he'd had a few; he's funniest when he's drunk.

Once we'd got to the top of the last set of stairs and emerged safe and sound on the street, we stopped to look at each other. It was a beautiful morning. He'd taken off his dark glasses, as if to help me recognise him.

"God, the light's blinding. I've been up all night."

His deep-set eyes were surrounded by heavy rings, he was fair-haired, with two-day-old stubble and a tooth missing. The moment he put his sunglasses back on I remembered his name and acknowledged my recognition with a mixture of pain and triumph. As I tugged out that name, many others came along, tangled up with it, not all of them so innocuous.

"Yeah, of course, Félix, it has been ages, at least eight years."

"That many? No shit. You haven't changed a bit. Why don't you buy me a coffee?"

"OK."

He hadn't asked if I was in a hurry, so I wasn't any more. It was refreshing to be with someone who didn't treat me with kid gloves or look at me with pity like my colleagues had been doing of late, someone to whom I could confess how sick I was of getting up early every morning and going to the same place every day, someone I could choose to tell everything or nothing, it wouldn't matter, rhizomorphs weren't known as especially careful listeners, and that was sometimes a good thing.

We went to a café he knew. We sat down. It was quite empty. He asked me if I was still writing songs.

"No. I'm an archivist now."

"How weird! Doesn't sound like you at all. How'd you wangle that, friends in high places?"

"No, I took the exams, spent two years studying for them, you'd never believe it. I wanted to make a living with a steady salary, I realised I needed it."

"Really? Did some psychiatrist tell you that?"

"Well, no, actually. It was a decision, like any other. And then the job turned out to have its own morbid fascination. Well, a fascination that's not your own, sometimes you're wandering around in the seventeenth century, at others you're hearing Second World War tanks roll by, but it's addictive."

Félix stared at me with watery eyes, that expression I know

so well, of someone pretending to understand but finding it a real effort.

"A fascination that's not your own," he echoed. "I like that. So you can take it or leave it."

"No, it's not that. You drown your own indecisiveness in that of others and forget about the mess your life's in. The same thing probably happens to firemen, doctors, lawyers – they probably wouldn't know how to sort themselves out, but still manage to serve humanity. Any profession that obliges you to get involved in something else – anything else – takes you away from your own scene, but if you do it well there are compensations. You put out a fire, mend a soul or a body, win an argument, reconstruct a dead person's past from their papers; whatever it is, other people's affairs, I mean. It's calming and you aren't implicated. They become your scene."

"OK. If you look at it like that . . ."

Our coffees had appeared and Félix was stirring sugar into his with the handle of a spoon. He always did that, he copied it from Roque. Roque isn't strictly speaking a rhizomorph. We all imitated him or tried to earn his admiration. I asked after him.

"He's living with Paula, I'm meeting them later. They're involved in something to do with advertising design. He invents other things as well, so he doesn't get too bogged down in all that shit. And so he can keep pretending to be someone else."

"What sort of things?"

He smiled, and his smile aged him, like all those gestures that reveal the deterioration of youthful fervour.

"Who knows? His imagination runs wild. I always tell Paula: let him go, he has to get out on the streets, give him a bit of respect, you know, how can you come out with this couple drivel at this stage? Roque's Roque, that's all there is to it. In short, he's pretty fucked up."

"Any particular reason?"

"Her kids and stuff, you know. Same thing happens to me with one I've got out there somewhere. It's a drag, no matter how much you say 'they'll get along', no matter how far away they are, kids stay alive and keep asking for Coca-Colas, there's no escaping it. And the whole mess gets to you, how can I put it, they get a hold of your ankles, your gut – you got any kids?"

"No."

"Well, lucky you."

I remembered Paula and her expensive perfume that smelled of roses. Her skin was very white and she had a Grecian profile, she'd married a blond aristocrat when she was very young and they used to throw parties at one of his father's country houses. I never went to one, but I heard there was a swimming pool with lights inside and at night everyone went skinny dipping.

Without skipping a beat, Félix started telling me the plot of a short film he was making with some friends, though the idea was his, about a guy who poisons his flatmate when he finds out she's going to have a baby. He insisted on the ambiguity of the message, it could be taken as his terror of bringing a new being into the world, as cowardice, or as jealousy, because the guy wasn't sure if it was him who'd got the girl pregnant; the first image was going to be the face of the dead woman, her expression slightly hateful, slightly rebellious, it had to be really feminist. Feminism sells.

"I wouldn't be so sure these days," I said. "And also, I'm sorry, but how do you figure you're going to make a feminist film about a guy who knocks off his girlfriend because she's pregnant?"

"Well, he suffers too."

"And how are you going to portray that? It sounds pretty confused to me, very confused."

It was quite a complicated psychological process, he agreed. The important thing was to provoke uncertainty in the spectator, it depended more on expressions than words, he was going to play the male lead. He was wondering whether to include the autopsy on the corpse. What did I think? The trouble was that it couldn't be more than ten minutes long.

"A bit of a limited format," I said, "for so many nuances and ups and downs, it seems more like material for a novel."

Félix shrugged his shoulders and looked off into space, as if the wind had suddenly gone out of his sails.

"Yeah," he said, "it's always the same. What we all really want is to write a novel and nab one of those big cash prizes and have our photograph taken with chin resting on hand."

We were sitting by a window and I recognised the street. On the other side was a Burger King with its yellow sign. I asked Félix if that wasn't exactly where *Fuego Fatuo* used to be, one of our old locals that stayed open until very late; I used to get out of bed sometimes on nights of embittered insomnia, when Roque had first stopped paying attention to me or showing up at the blue-papered garret. I'd sometimes grab a taxi and go down there to see if I could find him, I'd waltz in acting indifferent – hi guys – and often he wasn't there or he'd already left or no-one knew anything, *Fuego Fatuo* . . . it had a long bar with car headlights embedded in it.

"Yeah, that's where it was," said Félix. "The bars change so much in Madrid. Roque says the letters fall off the signs as if they were teeth, and it's the first symptom of encroaching gum disease."

I looked at the clock and told him I had to get going. I felt like a hole was piercing my insides. Félix asked if he could use that song of mine, "Living's the Strange Thing", as the soundtrack for his film, and where could he find it, it had a lot of pull, a rock number, wasn't it?

"Sort of, but very much in its own style. I called everything I did 'inter-rock', I don't know if you remember."

I could see he didn't remember, but he didn't say so. Nor could

I guess to what extent he'd known quite how much Roque had made me lose my footing back then, or if we were even associated in his memory. It didn't matter, after all. He repeated that it was a great song and he'd love to have a copy.

"Here, give me your address and I'll send you a copy of the cassette, if I can find it. I never did record the album. Not that one or any others."

"No? Oh, I didn't know. Well, I'll give you two phone numbers so you can track me down, I'm in the middle of moving."

He handed me two numbers written on a paper napkin, I paid and we said goodbye.

"Oh, one more thing," he said when we were outside. "Can you lend me 5,000 pesetas? As soon as we get the film made, I'll pay you back. I'm running on empty."

"Five thousand seems a lot, you know. Here, I'll give you 2,000."

He said he could get by on that and it'd been great to see me again.

"You look fantastic, too. Going through those files obviously agrees with you. Or is there something else?"

"There is a certain Tomás."

"Aha, I knew it. Never fails. Extra vitamins."

As I reached the Archive, I was thinking that Félix hadn't recanted, while I, on the other hand, had; and if I hadn't answered the call of the woods that morning, his name would have stayed hidden in the rhizomorph undergrowth. I was also reflecting that, in the days of "Living's the Strange Thing", there weren't any CDs yet and people had record players in their homes; my mother had one with really good sound, she'd sit on the floor between the speakers and listen to opera with her eyes closed.

And I already knew, as well, that the tide of other people's papers, where I went each day to drink in oblivion, would change in the foamy wake of that phantom ship.

Of course, I arrived late. Almost an hour after I should have started. With a stomach ache. And without the slightest desire to do any work.

IV

Archival Breeding Ground

The summer heat arrived overnight. I don't know if that contributed to my increased impatience. I'd get home in the early evening and before going into the bathroom, having a drink of water or feeding the cat, go straight to the answering machine. Nothing. Not a single message from the tall man. I listened to the others, usually Tomás, or messages for him, in the hope that the beep that ended each one would give way to the voice that had said to me: "depends on your capacity to play dangerous games", a voice my memory couldn't manage to reproduce but that my tendency to metaphor associated with a metallic-blue colour. I would shower, put on a pair of shorts, and once the sun had set, go out on the balcony for a moment to water, with neither enthusiasm not conviction, the pots in which oleander and geraniums languished. What I found most tiresome was knowing I was being watched by a similarly occupied neighbour, so I carried out my task without looking around, as if immersed in thought. Then, for four hours, nothing, a flat line on the encephalogram, my activity reduced to moving from armchair to sofa, skimming the newspaper and looking at my feet, which I rested on an enormous cushion.

The version of events circulating by telephone down to the Sierra de Cazorla was that I was making a lot of progress on my doctoral thesis: *An 18th-century Adventurer and His Servant*. Detained by order of Floridablanca in 1785, en route from London, on suspicion of being involved in a certain conspiracy led by some Jesuits expelled from Chile and Paraguay, all very bizarre, the master is named Luis Vidal y Villalba; the alleged servant, Juan de Edad, 27 years old, single, Puerto Rican (elsewhere mentioned as Juan Delage, from Bordeaux), claims to have met his master in Curaçao and to have served him since 1780. It's clear they both lie, especially Don Luis, who pretends to be Italian although he was Catalan, but that is discovered slowly; the government of Carlos III, tipped off from Paris by the Count of Aranda, believes Vidal to be very dangerous, a suspicion he encouraged by exaggerating his contacts and influences in private conversations, determined to live out his poor life as if it were a spy novel. For this he paid dearly with 20 years in prison. He claimed to own important properties in Martinique.

On 13 June 1785, San Antonio's feast day, a royal scribe goes to Las Rozas to await Don Francisco Gamir, "who was coming with a team of cavalry escorting a prisoner, who claims to be called Luis Vidal y Villalba". Don Francisco hands over the prisoner's personal effects to the governor of the Royal Prison, among them an oval miniature of a woman in a wooden frame, inside a little box also made of wood. Around the same time they go to wait for Juan de Edad at Galapagar, and he is imprisoned as well, but kept incommunicado from his master. During the initial interrogations he pretends to be mad.

I'd get so caught up in telling Tomás about the vicissitudes of that story, and about how my siege upon its enigmas was advancing, that when we'd hung up the phone I'd take notes on what I'd said, and it was the only time of the day when reality had another aroma, twisting excitedly in a salty breeze as birds took flight.

"Sounds like a novel," Tomás would say. "It's a shame you can't write it like a novel. Are you sure you didn't make up the little wooden box?"

"No, honest, I've got the notes in front of me. You don't realise what a wealth of information archival papers contain, the crazy things you can find in them, the only trouble is that you then have to put two and two together and guess what really happened, just like a police investigation. And structure it, of course."

"Just tell it like you've been telling me."

"The things you come out with! That wouldn't be a doctoral thesis."

"Forget about whether it's a thesis or not, for the millionth time, get a notebook and start putting it all down in a rough draft, as you discover things, then work from that. Start with that big notebook I brought you from Bordeaux, remember?"

"Of course, the green one, I've got it here."

Only the first page of the notebook was written on. It said: "An 18th-century Adventurer and His Servant", in shaded capital letters, and the date, January of that same year, when it wouldn't have occurred to anyone that my mother might die. And, when I thought about it, above those shaded capitals loomed that other immense shadow. I would thank Tomás for encouraging me so much from afar, pass on the odd message, we'd talk about the heat, I'd promise to start writing in the notebook. I was very pleased that I'd managed to spark his interest. Sometimes I wondered what would become of me if Tomás stopped being interested in the things I tell him, and the things I hide. Possibly a catastrophe.

By then it would usually be night-time. I wouldn't feel like going out or phoning anyone, the heat barely let up, it was a very cruel week. I'd look at my scattered papers, put them in order, label the folders I kept them in as I tidied them away; I'd find things I'd completely forgotten – that the servant was illiterate, for example, or that Don Luis had enticed him with promises of fortune worthy of those drawn up by Don Quixote for Sancho Panza – and for a while the interrogations of Don Blas de Hinojosa, *Consejero de Castilla*, in charge of turning the screws on those two prisoners in their separate cells, as disturbing and pertinacious as the contradictions they kept falling into, took over the summer and dispelled my apathy.

It wasn't just that I could see the golden thread of that investigation, but that I seemed to spend the whole evening absorbed in writing it out, active, stimulated, promising myself that the next day I'd look for more material, because many facts remained obscure. (More than two years have gone by since then and still obscure points proliferate, who knows if I'll finish the research one day, I never consider it settled or forgotten.)

The advantage of working in an archive is that you can photocopy documents and look through them slowly in your spare time, although there's not much spare time in the summer. Foreign scholars visit Spain in greater numbers between May and August. I tend to get along well with them, and they often end up telling me secrets about the characters whose trails they're following, as if they were relatives, sometimes rather trying ones, whom they've come to visit from Oklahoma, Toulouse or Melbourne – it's infuriating how their holiday or sabbatical year slips through their fingers, at the beginning they thought they'd make better use of the time, here in Spain life has a different rhythm – and I smile at them distantly or less so, depending on the mood I'm in or the impression they make. I'm friendlier with a few.

My most vivid recollection is of a professor from the Sorbonne whose subject was the state of the Spanish clergy at the end of the 18th century, particularly in relation to a bishop from Mondoñedo, accused of illicit love affairs. It was when I'd just passed my exams. We became friends and one day he invited me to lunch at an inexpensive restaurant in Argüelles. His biggest problem when he consulted a file – he said – was his inability to be interested in only one of the many stories that confronted him among that heap of papers; to restrict himself to his own story, to look and see if the material had anything to do with his – why his story, he wondered, who'd decided it was his? – and he knew from the moment he untied and unwrapped the records that he was going to get involved, distracted from the question that had brought him there by other stories he couldn't resist glancing through. In life the same thing happened, it was so impoverishing – he said – having to adhere so rigidly to what you'd chosen, rejecting anything else as merely an interesting possibility but nevertheless having to accept it, we spend our lives making choices, as much as it overwhelms us, we're condemned to do so, our thirst for infinity banging against the bars of our cage; *c'est la vie*, he sighed. He had a grey beard and blue eyes. His wife had died three years earlier and he had a son and a daughter more or less my age, he guessed, looking at me. I asked him if he had thought of marrying again. He said no, he didn't like women of his age and he wouldn't want to subject a younger woman to the progressive deterioration of dealing with an obsessive. Moreover, he'd truly loved his wife, he missed her a lot; he'd been unfaithful a couple of times but often wondered wistfully what things would have been like if he'd never met her, he couldn't resist the temptation of imagining it, with a sort of perverse pleasure, it's so unfair that life forces us to make exclusive choices, you go in one door and then there's only one corridor that gets darker and darker with doors at the end through which you also must pass, ever narrower and more imperious.

I felt a knot in my stomach; I'd stopped writing songs and drinking like there was no tomorrow by then, I'd met Tomás and found the door to the Archive, through which I passed daily, I had the feeling I was at the beginning of that long corridor. I looked at my companion as if he might offer some consolation. He was smiling.

"Good thing I believe in reincarnation," he said.

"Do you?"

"Oh yes. Absolutely," he said seriously. "Don't you?"

"I'm not sure. I have thought about it. Living's so strange that you can expect absolutely anything, if you're expecting something, that is."

He looked at me very tenderly, as I imagined he'd look at his daughter. "Didn't you read fairy tales when you were little?"

"Of course, I still do, they're what make most sense to me. And that's precisely why: because I find the fact that an animal speaks and tells us, for example, that he's under a spell and he's actually another being to be the most normal thing in the world. Thanks for mentioning fairy tales. They're the subconscious. I have dreams sometimes where I am transformed too, and things happen inside me, do you know what I mean, I witness transformations, and I say, 'Now they'll see me with another face,' you'll think that's strange . . ."

I'd started to feel sad. I didn't know why I was talking to a stranger in this way. I had an instantaneous but scorching desire: I wanted to ask him to be my father and take me with him to Paris. It would be going down a different corridor.

"It doesn't seem strange to me, *ma belle*. In the end, everything is metamorphosis. What have you turned into now? A captive princess or a talking cat? Come on, make a wish."

I started to laugh so he wouldn't see that I felt like crying.

"You're much younger than lots of 25-year-old guys," I told him.

And then, because it was quite a noisy restaurant, I stood up to ask them to please turn down the volume on the television. When I came back he'd made a flower out of a paper napkin, he put a bit of salt on it and held it out over the table to me with a Chaplinesque gesture.

Over dessert, the conversation returned to the hidden treasures of historical research, and that was when he told me about

Vidal y Villalba, a complete stranger to me. It's a shame – he said – that no-one's investigating that story, he'd found it entangled in the papers of the Bishop of Mondoñedo and it was sure to conceal many mysteries. For one thing, during their interrogation in the prison, neither Vidal nor his servant appeared to utter a single truthful word. At first I wasn't even interested, truthful word about what a I didn't get it. And I was incensed that the thread of intimacy – which for a moment had sewn my real story to that of someone who might in another life have been my father, and who was now meticulously cutting his peaches in syrup into little pieces, while telling me about two extravagant, obscure convicts – had snapped.

"OK, but why did they arrest them?"

"There's the question. I think in 1785 Carlos III and his ministers got itchy fingers at the slightest whiff of any plot threatening their authority in the American colonies. In fact, they asked Vidal several times whether he'd met the Inca Tupac Amaru, Chief of Tinta, during his time in the Philippines and Peru, or if he knew anything about him; apparently they weren't satisfied with having inflicted such a horrible death on the chief three years earlier, they feared the seed of his fleeting revolution. And they were right to. It was the first time the harshness and tyranny of the Spanish *corregidores* in the colonies was protested with blood and fire, as I'm sure you know."

No. I didn't know, but it was getting late, I had to get back to work, and the names Tupac Amaru and Vidal y Villalba had become forever connected in my mind. I'd decided I wanted to delve a little further into those stories.

We said goodbye at the entrance to the metro, because we were going in opposite directions, and he was leaving the next day. He left me a card with his name, Ambroise Dupont, and his address in Paris. I've sometimes thought to write to him, but then I think what for, to fill my cupboards with obsolete papers? He also gave me the number of the file in which he'd found those remnants of research.

"In case you decide to follow it up, wistful girl. Rummaging around in the distant past can be soothing. The recent past hurts more."

We kissed goodbye and I stood watching him go down the steps to enter his own particular woods. Then, when I got back to the Archive, I began to look through that file before putting it away, purely out of curiosity, intrigued by Monsieur Dupont, a blue-eyed widower I've never seen since. He'll have gone through other doors by now or transformed into someone else, that's the way life is.

So I met Vidal y Villalba in a cheap restaurant in Argüelles and followed his trail because of my mania for going down to the woods, to all the woods; it would never have occurred to me to write a thesis with the first attempts at colonial independence in the 18th century as its background, nor do I think I'll ever write it, but anyway, the story of the two obscure extras, Don Luis and his servant, continues to drag on, sometimes buried and sometimes rearing its head again, incomplete, a sporadic story like so many that concern me more directly, and somehow amalgamated with them.

I've thought of Ambroise Dupont many times since then, not only the paper flower and the fairy tales but also because he was so right when he said that it's absurd to take an interest only in one matter out of the many that appear to waylay us in archival papers and in life.

The person I really fell in love with at first sight was José Gabriel Tupac Amaru. But there was no sense in doing a doctoral thesis on him, because there were already so many books about the fate of the Chief of Tinta. I didn't stop till I'd read them all.

Perhaps if one day I really decide to write up my work on the lying adventurer and his servant, the most scintillating opening would be the appearance of Tupac Amaru in the first chapter, as a heroic counterpart to the sordid Don Luis. When I think of it, I seem to hear the hooves of his white horse galloping across a river as he escapes enemy fire.

V

Other-worldly Guests

During those first days of July, as I waited for the tall man's call, I thought a lot about death. But in a stunned, abstract way, like a persistent drumming, a backdrop with pictures commissioned by pharaohs to commemorate their dead. What struck me as most strange was that I'd so quickly grown used to thinking of my mother as someone who would never again feel hot in the summer or lean out at night to look at the rooftops of Madrid; as someone who belonged as much to the past as Vidal y Villalba. She doesn't hear any more – I'd say to myself – and even if I asked her she can no longer explain anything, she can't lie or defend herself any more, she's tiptoed away with her secrets, with her inscrutable expression, she'll no longer suffer from the heat; and she took with her the part of my childhood that was entangled in her skein. I didn't think "she'll take it", as I had when, on other occasions, I'd imagined, with a start, her absence, but rather "she took it". I thought of it as something inexorable. And the umbilical cord of untold stories became covered in rust.

To say "she took part of my childhood" was to picture myself flying in her still-young arms towards a remote place – my games and my questions interrupted, atlases left open, Parcheesi counters left out, the puzzle half-finished, coloured pencils with broken tips, the bike on its side, "hurry!" – and a whirlwind would sweep us off the floor up into the air "come on, don't be scared, hold on tight"; it was like a spaceship, but I knew that soon it would plummet, deep into the bowels of the earth, and I'd close my eyes, trembling.

When I opened them again, the vibration of motorbikes and buzz of conversation drifted up from the darkened street. This is a neighbourhood with lots of pubs, open-air bars and commotion, those background noises kept me company, decorating an urban novel with no intriguing ending, I'd read that novel a thousand times, and I'd seen the movie. I could dress up in disguise, go down and ask for a part, look for whoever's in charge of casting, do a screen test, I've got nerve, good reflexes and can dodge a knife, I can hold my liquor, know how to improvise a quick retort, and if the script requires it, I'll take my clothes off, even in Cibeles, let me do a screen test, OK, let's see, are you wearing a bra, how boring, I already know the whole story. I turned on the television with a sigh, poured myself a whisky, furtively stroked the cat and missed Tomás furiously. But I was determined to hold out, I'd decided that this matter was mine alone; it was my childhood that lay mutilated on the carpet, it would need artificial resuscitation or maybe even an autopsy, search for photos, papers, remember how she dressed, the expression she used to hide her anger: prepare myself, in a word, for my conversation with my grandfather, because the tall man could be about to order me on to the stage. I knew that as soon as I heard his voice I'd be inspired, it was that kind of voice. But, meanwhile, where was Mum?

The idea of a total disappearance wasn't part of my acceptance of her death, nor were calculations of how much time had gone by since the day they'd given me the news – two months, three? – that didn't matter, what counted was the solid wall erected since then, forever, between her voyage and my own. What she took: where did she take it?

I hadn't wanted to see her corpse, I'd barely even wanted to ask what she died of, the funeral struck me as a pastiche, I went in dark glasses and jeans. Rosario, her flatmate, went in mourning and cried so much that people offered her their condolences. My father, in his way, was very affectionate, although shy. I asked him not to phone me for a few days, "I'll call you if I need anything, if you don't mind, OK?" And he seemed to understand – he takes off his glasses and rubs his eyes when he's understood something – he said, "But don't leave me alone for too long," a phrase that seemed to spring from his heart, completely unexpected, I think Montse heard because she was standing nearby and she frowned, anyway, I didn't know what she was doing there, but at least she hadn't brought their little boy. I spent that evening with music blaring, while I listened to Tomás answering the phone and excusing me, asking people not to come over; darling man, I think his mother was scandalised when she heard those chords of strident rock, she couldn't deal with it, "everyone feels things in their own way, don't be so conventional, Mum, please"; since then she's been angry with him and also with me, because she thinks I'm a bad influence, how anecdotal all this is, how inconsistent and shoddy. It distracts from the fundamental. It's so boring.

And the tall man didn't phone.

I managed to keep from calling there, if only to find out his name, for two days. When I phoned, I said it was in order to invite him to a conference on Geriatrics. "Ramiro Núñez," intoned the nasal voice of the woman with the tightly pulled back hair who'd received me at the entrance desk. And I hung up straight away with my heart pounding. But I didn't dare try anything else.

Sometimes it annoyed me to think that in rhizomorph days I would have done whatever it took to bridge the gap between my desire to see him again and its consequence; back then I would stop at nothing to give my body pleasure. And, when it came down to it, Ramiro Núñez was a body thing, he was someone who had inopportunely awoken my appetite for pleasure. That was it, wasn't it? "Well, slow down, there's more to it than that," I reasoned in my moments of lucidity, "don't forget that she and Grandfather were the indisputable stars of the story you're so keen to monopolise, heading the cast; and for that reason your rôle is not going to be an easy one, it will require subtlety and much preparation. Sure, they might give you an Oscar for Best Supporting Actress, take it or leave it, but tone down your ego. Ramiro isn't a predictable director, you know, he's testing you from afar without divulging his game. Besides, isn't that what you like about him? Well, loosen up your neurons. If you call him, compel him to make some approach, you've lost, it would be like killing the hen that lays the golden eggs."

At other times, I fooled myself that I felt a concern for my grandfather that wouldn't take long to reveal itself as false. What if something happened to him before I went to see him?

But I had to confess that this had nothing to do with mollifying supposed pangs of conscience, or keeping company with a rather tyrannical old man of whom I'd washed my hands quite a while ago and everything to do with whether to accept the risks entailed in this particular challenge, laid down by a stranger who I wasn't even sure was interested in me as a woman. But perhaps it didn't matter. It was an adventure, even without that. And if I got involved – which I already was – it had to be on top form, with absolutely no risk of defeat due to ignorance.

"Think it through. We need you to use all five senses or it won't work at all," Ramiro had said when we parted.

"We need." That plural included her, who else? And although I hadn't exactly realised its significance when I'd heard it, thinking of that detail later made my hair stand on end. They were accomplices, no doubt about it.

I answered him: "Of course. One does these things properly

or not at all, if you knew me you wouldn't feel you had to tell me that."

But it had been a bluff, that was clear now. I wasn't getting ready to take Mum's place at all, I didn't dare take on that rôle. I didn't dare mess with her, frankly, because despite all my rebelliousness, I'd never dared try to knock her off her pedestal.

And that background music, the tom-tom drums of the unknown, struck up again: the enigma of her present whereabouts.

"Where are you?" I asked in a low voice with my eyes screwed up and hands in the air, imitating a gesture halfway between comic and serious that, according to her, accompanied the sound of my first babyish "Where?".

I came in from the balcony to the bedroom in shadow and stood in front of the mirror, "Where?", and looking at my silhouette framed by the light from the rooftops gave a ghostly certainty to that gesture of a curious little girl, relived by way of an imitation of the woman who had described a scene played out by me, which was stored away with my own memories as if I'd seen it myself, along with all the borrowings, testimony and sidelong versions that hold life together; it is in this way, based on disparate fragments, that memory is forged and destiny repaired. It would seem that "Where?" was my first word, "very clear, hurriedly drawing out the *e*, as if your life depended on finding out, and you weren't just asking about some specific 'where', you were looking around in every direction, you were so funny, it seemed like an investigation of the world in general."

In the darkened mirror, lit only by the reddish lights that came in from the open door to the balcony, my orphaned image slowly lifted her hands up high, I saw her sink to her knees, "do this in memory of me," I closed my eyes as if under the influence of a magical potion, awaiting some transformation or wonderful revelation – Where? – I whispered. Where is she now, the one who told me, from whom I inherited my talent to imitate other people's voices? Because she must have ended up somewhere, that's for sure, although we wouldn't see each other again, although they'd interrogate us in separate cells, like Vidal y Villalba and his servant.

I opened my eyes on the messy, tedious, rarefied bedroom. And behind that sort of ritual, concluded with disappointment, loomed a disturbing concept that had eaten away at me when I was little and that resurfaced later during my Art History studies, especially when I contemplated reproductions of Egyptian or Assyrian tombs: the world beyond.

It's impossible not to imagine this realm somehow, all religions have done, and resolving the issue by saying it's all nonsense won't do. Since those nights at the beginning of July when I waited for the tall man to call on me to perform, the guardian of the world beyond has had the face of Robert De Niro for me, due to a very strange film I saw on television in the early hours, already half-asleep; I don't remember what it was called or what it was about, but he stuck in my mind. He appears with his hair parted and slicked back, long fingernails, a treacherous look, eating a hard-boiled egg. He became encrusted on my imaginings that night like a limpet, like a bird drawn on a funereal frieze, I recognised him immediately and he left his own film to get into mine, he's still in it, he looked like he could be doing guard duty at the border. I didn't want to know more. I turned off the television.

I imagine the world beyond as a kind of huge warehouse, heaving and rough, parts of it open to the elements, other parts roofed over. Sometimes I've gone there in dreams, dreams where naturally I'm dead too.

And there you find yourself with people who send you to someone else or turn into someone else, who you remember vaguely or not at all, people who greet you with the slightest of nods, eyes staring and serious; they don't want to remember their stories or for anyone else to mention them, they've decided to auction off the remains of the past and all traces of hope. They generally wear hats. They stand or sit still, with their few belongings in front of them like in the market, and they're recognisable by these objects, but nobody buys anything. Don Luis Vidal y Villalba offers his closed wooden box with the woman's portrait inside, he doesn't remember who she was any more, he's incapable of separating lies from truths, his skin is yellow from his last fevers and delirium, poor man, he came to a terrible end in a cell on the Rock of Gibraltar, his reason entirely lost, but he no longer remembers. Nobody buys anything, no, nor do they know why they carry these things around with them – postcards tied up with ribbon, portraits, keys, a tortoiseshell glasses case, bundles of various things – but they've gone around grabbing these residues of forgotten identities through the halls and corridors and crags of the world beyond, lost, stumbling, seeking a hollow of calm.

Here, we keep ourselves tenaciously involved in a series of misguided, baroque formalities that have nothing to do with their confinement or loss. There, they advance with great difficulty, trying not to collide with each other, across this lunar landscape that Robert De Niro guides them through, maybe he tells them to take the metro and gives them a map of the various lines, stops and transfer points.

Every once in a while they see concentration camps with fluorescent lights shining from them, these are the refugees who've been here for more than five centuries, from the time of the Reconquest of Granada and before.

The investigator of all these deaths, attempting to go down and nose around, is also met by Robert De Niro with his long fingernails, his slicked-back hair and his solemn mourning suit.

"Investigation, scheduled excursion or mere formality?" he asks with his sardonic smile.

"Investigation."

He hands you a black ticket on which is written in yellow letters: "Abandon all hope. The dead must be left to make their own way."

VI

Tell Me Whatever

"Something's up with you," Tomás said. "You're going off on tangents just like you did when I first met you."

His tone of voice was rather like a specialist confronting the reappearance of symptoms that change the clinical prognosis and put paid to an initial improvement. The iris of my untempered narratives was dazzled.

"You say that as if it worried you. Are you worried?"

There was a silence at the other end of the line. If Tomás has one virtue – and in fact he has many – it's that he never answers just for the sake of it. It's what both keeps me in check and serves as an antidote, although his determination to be specific sometimes makes me nervous. I saw storm clouds gathering.

"I asked you a question," I said impatiently.

"I heard you, I'm thinking. You know that telephone explanations aren't my forte. Never mind at this hour. I'm not worried, exactly. Well, I don't think that's it. Besides, it's to do with you, not me, as it almost always is. Whether it feels OK to you or not."

"Whether *what* feels OK to me or not? You sound like a doctor. Tell me whatever it is, come on."

I heard a little sound, the clicking of his tongue, like boredom. When I say "tell me whatever it is" it's an expression of vulnerability and, as imploring as it might sound, he and I both know that it doesn't offer an opening in the dialogue, but is more like the defensive gesture of a cat arching its back. I was cross with myself for having said it, but I needed to invent another mountain for my rage to scale. For example, his silence, which continued.

"Are you still there?"

"Yes."

"What did you say? Did you sigh?"

"No, actually. But it's a good idea." He sighed audibly.

I looked at the clock. It was 1.15 in the morning. I'd phoned to ramble on about something that had occurred to me while I was half-asleep, something to do with Robert De Niro and his other-worldly guests, without asking Tomás if I'd woken him or whether or not he found it utterly captivating to listen to me talk nonsense. I'm inconsiderate, I admit it, or rather, I admit it without grace, as with almost everything that doesn't become me. He was leaving me more or less alone now; it seemed that the job had got complicated and he couldn't come back to Madrid as soon as he'd thought, but he'd stopped insisting I go and visit him. That sigh was like a knife, and it made me imagine the unimaginable: that he might be in bed with another woman. Naturally I wasn't going to ask him, total liberty in that field had been agreed since the beginning, and nevertheless I took it for granted that Tomás never made use of that freedom. Why? This was based on rash confidence and nothing more. Why couldn't it happen? Hadn't I spent several nights tempted to go out and hook up with someone, remembering Roque and dreaming about Ramiro Núñez? And that was leaving aside certain earlier infidelities that remained more or less unconfessed. I still haven't guessed if Tomás is jealous or not; he reveals little of his soul, all I've figured out is that it's not turbulent like mine.

"There are no strict rules about that," he said once. "If I betrayed you, I'd tell you. You can do what you want." I made a joke of his solemn tone. "The word *betrayal* has to be spoken soundlessly, didn't you know, as in silent movies, eyes bulging, hand on heart, you have to put on a Mary Pickford mouth, look, like this." He kissed me, laughed a lot and said why didn't I take up acting. That was at the beginning.

But would he really tell me if it happened? Or would he have a different view of betrayal now? Although he didn't normally change his opinion without explanation, though I didn't give him much of an outlet, I sidetracked conversations on a whim, which can be tiresome. With his sigh Tomás had just added another suffocating degree to the foul air the fan was pushing lazily across the bed, which was deformed from so many successive visits and desertions, the whole thing a heap. The air-conditioning unit had been broken for days, I needed to get someone to come and fix it, but it seemed vulgar to think so much about the heat, and to blame it for my nerves, like something out of a cheap farce. Tomás wasn't suffering from the heat in Cazorla or at least he didn't go on about it, and nevertheless he'd sighed with eloquence, I imagined him pouting, he has a lovely mouth, a shy one, which is better without a moustache.

I felt the notion that he might not be sleeping alone settle furtively, like a poisonous insect, and I lay in wait, now it was crawling up the bedspread, making its way between the piles of debris scattered around, it was getting close to the telephone, I squashed it with a magazine, a hairy spider stuck to Stephanie of Monaco's cleavage, dead it scared me more. I needed something to drink.

"Tomás," I said sweetly. "Wait a second, OK? Don't hang up on me."

I heard a slight rustle as if he were changing position, I was at a disadvantage in not knowing his room. He tends to fall asleep reading the paper.

"Hang up on you? When have I ever done that?" he asked in a tone halfway between reticent and long-suffering, which revived my barely numbed appetite for a fight. "That's not my style, as you may recall."

"But it is mine, isn't it! And slamming doors, and waking you up mercilessly and steamrollering and changing the subject and never listening to you, you're perfect, I agree, a measured and rational being, what I don't understand is how you put up with such a hysteric."

The flourish would be for me to hang up, but I didn't, and another swampy silence ensued, this time an unbearable one; if I didn't want the spider to come back to life, I needed to get my wits together and invent an amusing pirouette to get us out of this hole, what I needed most was to hear him laugh, I knew it. My throat was dry, I felt nauseated and my legs were asleep, but I prepared to take the leap. He wasn't going to. I know his capacity to endure embarrassing situations.

"Huuuuuuugh!" I sighed exaggeratedly, stretching it out into a howl. "I'm getting all Dostoyevsky, aren't I?"

"Well, yeah. You say sorry like you're throwing stones."

"But don't be so serious, come on, can't you see I'm trying to damp down the flames a little bit? Let's say goodnight without leaving things charred. Repeat after me: 'You're getting all Dostoyevsky.' That'll do it."

He laughed a little, though without much enthusiasm. Or maybe he didn't want to make his companion jealous. Laughing with someone is the primary symptom of love.

"You're getting all Dostoyevsky," he said.

"All right then, goodnight. And forgive me. I'm a wreck in this heat. Really, no sane person would stay in Madrid these days."

It would have been logical for him to reply: "So, why don't you come down here?", or more belligerently: "You do have a choice," but it was clear he had no desire to prolong the polemic.

"Anyway," he said with a note of suspicion, "I assume they've been to fix the air-conditioning."

I told him they had, although it was a lie, and the pressing matter of calling the Panasonic people resurfaced, increasing my disquiet. I had little notes pinned up in every room to remind me, and I was sick of seeing them. He asked me if it was quiet now and I said yes and he said goodnight without any further comment. The spider moved its legs a little.

"Just one question, Tommy," I said before hanging up. "Isn't it true that when we first met you liked me because of the way I went off on tangents and sewed the truth together with threads of lies? That metaphor's your invention, not mine. Maybe you disavow it now."

"No, no, I don't disavow anything. But don't start obsessing over those stories again, or anything else that might overwhelm you. Come on, take a sleeping pill and start that notebook on Vidal y Villalba tomorrow."

"All right, boss."

He waited for me to hang up first. I was having trouble breathing, but most of all I was very hungry, and an earlier expedition to the fridge had revealed its emptiness. I scorned half a glass of whisky with melted ice and decided to head out to the Residuo bar where the kitchen stayed open late and the owners were really nice. I'd gone for days eating terribly and going overboard on the alcohol and coffee.

As I took off my pyjamas and grabbed some clothes thrown over an armchair, I realised with alarm that I was repeating the scene for the third time that evening. Oh no, well now, honey, you're not going to stop before you finish it – I admonished myself out loud – three strikes and you're out, that's enough of "making indecisions" like your father, whom you resemble in that respect.

I smiled. "Ismael, don't make any more indecisions today." She used to say that, before they separated that is, because afterwards she rarely mentioned him for better or for worse; I would have been about 16, or younger? I didn't want to dredge up any dates, but that phrase surfacing like a drowned man led me to "make the indecision" to visit my father the next day. I wrote down on a piece of yellow notepaper – "Visit Dad" – and stuck it on the bathroom mirror on top of another one that said "Panasonic". I pulled my hair back and put on a bit of eyeliner. My face looked awful, like that of a wicked woman in an old movie.

Suddenly I sort of split in two, as if I'd lost my identity as Tomás's partner, yet still moved with ease through that house I knew well, and to which I had a key. It was strange, I had come here for one night, I was pretty drunk, Tomás much less so. There was a huge drawing-board that isn't here any more, its slanted surface was the first thing you saw when the door opened, it was a place like any other, I thought, so why was I still here?

Another consignment of questions approached, questions related to before, after and meanwhile, questions I didn't want to ponder indoors.

Out, that's enough seclusion! The street will provide a fresh perspective, don't you know that by now, a pretext for going down into unexplored woods; the street where other people walk along lost in their own undergrowth; and especially since there's not a morsel left in the fridge and you're hungry, aren't you? Well then, hurry up before they close the Residuo, don't get caught up in any more vicious interior circles. What does it matter how you met Tomás? You need to have a hot meal. You can go over that stage of your life another time, if you think it's worth it.

I practically fled the house.

VII

Four Drops of Existentialism

The people who run the Residuo are a woman in her twenties, dark-haired with lots of ringlets, known as the Duchess, and two guys who are older than me. I don't know how much longer I'll keep calling them guys, Quique is bald now and has a bit of a paunch, Moisés carries it better – physically I mean, mentally, I'm not so sure. He used to have a beard. He's one of those people I've seen around for years without ever knowing his name or what he did for a living – on a University bus, at Tierno Galván's funeral, at those concerts where we used to hold up our lighters, queuing outside the Alphaville cinemas, at the anti-NATO demos, in Chicote – and eventually his blond beard started to go a bit grey and then he shaved it off. Back then I didn't know he had a bar and frankly, I wouldn't have guessed it, I thought he was a journalist or a professor, until a colleague of mine at the Archive who knows that cooking bores me, especially at night, told me about the Residuo, which is in her neighbourhood. Since then I've been quite often, sometimes with Tomás, but usually on my own. The two men are melancholic and discreet, she's a bit livelier, her name's Trilce. They don't have a television or a fruit machine. Trilce comes from a good Andalucian family fallen on hard times and she makes these delicious, really filling stews, her grandmother's recipes, an expertise developed in satisfying hordes of hungry grandchildren.

Trilce tells anecdotes about her grandmother at every opportunity, each new stew brings up one of Doña Amparo's stories or witticisms, it seems she was the one who had the idea of setting up this business. What I don't know is how Trilce met her associates, whom she teases with affection. The three of them live in an attic near the restaurant, but I don't think they're related.

As soon as I'd eaten a plate of rissoles and a slice of cheesecake, I felt a blunt tiredness come over me. I looked at the walls decorated with photographs of movie stars and jazz musicians and couldn't bear the thought that they might turn me out, not that I felt any less vulnerable floating adrift in that underwater atmosphere than I had at home, they must be getting ready to close, there was only one customer at the bar and another one at a table, no-one was talking, what have I got to do with this place or the stories of its owners? Who would miss me if I stopped coming?

Nevertheless, I had to admit how much worse it would be to be struggling right now to share my insomnia with Tomás in a temporary flat. It didn't really matter if he'd fallen asleep with his arms around a body other than mine, I even imagined the relief I'd feel, like at other times, when I'd slip out of his embrace and feel for any hole in the wall, anxious for a cocktail of stars. How sad, not a single bar nearby, no late-night pharmacy, everything closed, outside only darkness and trees moving their branches across the façade, the sound of a motorbike in the distance, and inside nothing, you don't expect a shelf of fortuitous books in this kind of refuge, not even a lousy table lamp, tacky décor, at most a minuscule fridge with tiny bottles and packets of almonds, they don't provide poison, they never take the client's needs seriously.

I looked at the green payphone at the back, enshrined in its plastic niche beside the corridor that led to the toilets, and it didn't say a thing to me or invite me to do anything. A connection to an imagined bedroom in the province of Jaén presented itself in its most ordinary and heartless guise, entirely without solace. So what did I want? It was one of those times when one feels disquiet mounting like an angry tide and knows that only through abandonment to its rolls and punches will the mind sharpen enough to see things so clearly that it will almost be frightening.

It's hard to accept how incidental we are, our inability to convey to each other anything more than travesties of vacillating souls; and to accept at the same time the gestures and babbling we stubbornly use to try to get close to those we've supposed form part of our stories. Hearing Tomás's voice bounce off mine had turned into a sort of venomous respiration, the air keeps being sucked in until the lung wastes away, but not before giving a few warnings of the danger and inconsistency of our effort. And this was one of those warnings.

"Do you feel like hearing a *fado*?" Moisés asked me from the bar. "You look like you could use a *fado*."

I snapped out of my abstraction to look at him. Everybody had left now. We were alone. But he didn't show any sign of turning me out, he was keeping me there. It was like the sun coming out.

"No, hey, how about some Caribbean music? And a coffee, please, I'm getting sleepy."

When he brought it over, the velvety voice of Benny Moré was playing. They had a great stereo system. He asked if he could sit with me. I nodded enthusiastically.

"It would be terrible," I said, "if you didn't really exist right now. Do you exist? Give me a kiss, let's see."

And, seeing his disconcerted expression, I added: "Sorry, effects of persistent claustrophobia; I couldn't leave the house, and I was desperate to. How long have I been here?"

"About an hour and a half," he said as he bent down to kiss me. "But don't worry."

"You're not going to kick me out, are you?"

"Of course not. I'm just going to lock up before I sit down.

Quique and Trilce have cashed up and gone home. But I could use a bit of a chat too. I'm not tired. When it comes down to it, we're all castaways. What's up? Is your boyfriend away?"

"Yes, but it's not that," I said quietly.

. . . And what was it? I wondered as I watched him lock up, his back to me, sure he hadn't heard. It was something. Tomás, sensing the shadows from afar, tossed his words back at me again: "Something's up with you." I hadn't wanted to focus on them at the time, it was me who steered the conversation off into a stupid quarrel. Well yes, something was up with me, something deep and dark like a landslide, and the still vague threat of it made me yearn for a port where I could sleep safe from all the toing and froing, drop anchor, but where? I didn't know of anywhere I could really trust, perhaps I had known such a place, but they were landscapes where wind didn't blow, brought to a halt in mislaid photographs, a garden with hammocks, an ivy-covered façade, a tin clown, a river, an office with a glowing fireplace, horses galloping, it had rained a lot on these images, they had blurred behind a curtain of ceaseless water, the universal flood.

"It's nice here at this time of night," said Moisés as he sat down. "It's been a hard day."

I smiled at him, afloat in that makeshift refuge. He'd made himself a daiquiri.

"Yeah," I said. "It sure has. Mostly due to the lack of secrets."

I say these things without thinking, Tomás calls them excrescences, I say them and they seem so strange to me that I don't usually expect a response. But Moisés had one.

"That's fantastic," he said. "You won't believe it, but not long ago I was thinking just that. Let's see, what are people really after, I was wondering while waiting on a table, a bored barman's question, because we've had a really common bunch in today, there was a match in Bernabeu, they came in all rowdy and thick, and I suddenly said to myself: 'They're after secrets,' just like that, in a flash, it seemed a good idea for a song or something, 'secret craving', and now you come out with the same thing, how strange, no?"

"It doesn't surprise me. Everything's strange, as soon as you start paying a bit of attention. Living's the strange thing. That we can be sitting here, that we can speak and be heard, put one sentence after another without looking at a single book, that nothing's hurting us, that what we drink goes down and knows when it has to swerve, that the air nourishes us while it doesn't nourish others any more, that we feel like doing something or its opposite according to our whims and that these whims probably depend on fate, it's all so much that you can't take it in, and the strangest thing is that it seems normal to us."

What I was telling him seemed unimportant all of a sudden, because an additional source of richness had been forming, flowing recklessly from Benny Moré's music and deafening the other one. I fell silent because I couldn't talk about so many things at the same time without first understanding them, I needed to concentrate on this new strangeness that had come over me. Benny Moré was said to have been a poor Cuban who caught hold of Creole rhythms as a way out of poverty, one of those biographies of uphill struggle and lots of rum – or maybe I was confusing him with another musician, I was pretty sure he was dead, but even if he wasn't the moment of his singing didn't coincide with that of his listeners in the Residuo. I pictured him singing in an open-air club to which I added stars, palm trees and the nearby pulse of a tropical beach; and couples looking each other in the eye, feeling the rhythm of their young bodies join with the music, something unarguable and liberating, where this is taking us, they thought, it's not going to stop, it can't stop. Date uncertain, live recording, applause could be heard after each song. That night, which had slipped away from its own time and into ours, could have given rise to the procreation of malnourished children who might now be flirting with delinquency in some South American country while their mothers grew older longing for that sensual, ardent dance.

For me, on the other hand, the advent of Benny Moré distanced me from my present companion, who, inspired by my comments on how strange it was to live, had begun to talk about Kierkegaard. I could have interrupted by asking him to dance with me or explaining what I was thinking, but too much talk can be dangerous and this special moment between Moisés and me suggested a leap I didn't at all feel like taking – his body didn't invite me to risk it, that was all. I imagined arriving home with him, taking the clothes and books off the unmade bed, dimming the light, apologising for not having anything to drink, maybe even telling him this wasn't my house, that I hadn't yet found my place in the world, and I was horrified. What makes you realise you don't want to take someone to bed? I don't know the answer, but there's no getting past it, there's a sudden flash and that's it. When I said: "Give me a kiss," I hadn't even considered the dilemma that was now behind us. For melting into Benny Moré, alive or dead, Moisés was of no use to me. Fortunately, he was showing no sign that might put me on my guard; we were travelling separate paths, and his was heading towards misty shapes: existentialist philosophy. He'd been at it for a while, as Benny passionately asked us to dance to his *son*.

Faced with the currents of Platonic thought that culminate in Hegel, attention begins to veer towards existence itself as the nucleus of philosophical speculation. I half-listened to him, drumming my fingers on the table, and when our eyes met the distance was accentuated. The first to pose the strangeness of living was Kierkegaard, he anticipated Sartre and Heidegger, but people now look at all that as a relic, have you noticed? And it's hugely topical.

Fine, I thought, he wants to show off or let off steam after the tedium of serving drinks all evening, and I understand; waiters seem heroic to me, I've always said so, I don't know how they can be friendly to us boring people who go out drinking. He confessed he'd never given up the idea of writing a book that focused on existentialist philosophy from a contemporary viewpoint, an idea cherished, and evolving, since his first years of university because the "contemporary" is constantly changing – didn't I think young people had become much more nihilistic? By the time he'd finished his degree he had a lot of material for the book, but the situation for drop-outs was different then, first of all because they weren't even called drop-outs yet, and then life takes you where you don't want it to, he'd had to take the first job that came up, what else could he do, there were a lot of brothers and sisters in a family without much money and reactionary to boot, "Shake my father," he said, "and acorns fall out, it's better not to argue or ask him for anything." He'd returned to the book project about a year ago now, he got up early and spent a couple of hours each morning at the National Library, the best part of the day, you get distracted at home, and besides he didn't have much willpower, he wanted to start from *The Concept of Anxiety* by Kierkegaard and bring it down to street level, which is where you can sense anxiety. "Well, you sense it at home, too," I said; but he didn't take that in, he kept on, sticking to his notes. Anxiety springs from the concept of mortality, he said, it all stems from there, from the fact that we're going to die, and when we think of it we find it strange, it's like alighting from the clouds. Lots has been written on the subject, of course – he concluded as the last strains of "Fiebre de ti" faded – but there's always room for an original and striking version, don't you think? And he looked at me for the first time, waiting for an opinion. I let the pause settle a bit.

"I think," I said, "that what would be most striking would be to hear the testimony of someone who'd already died, to see what they say, but it's difficult because they don't come back, only once in a while in dreams, and there's not always time to write down their words, because they talk, of course, but you forget, you say 'it was a dream' and yet at the same time you don't forget that you have to pay the telephone bill. The dead are the only ones who know how strange living was, they come to understand it when they can no longer recount it in any book."

Moisés remained silent and went to the bar to make himself another drink. The Benny Moré tape had finished and I started to get a little bored, I checked the time, look, you know, I'm going to get going, no, don't, we're having such a nice chat, what's your hurry, have a drink, I don't feel like one, but stay till I finish mine, OK, just a little while longer.

And Moisés came back and sat down across from me, without background music now. The worst thing, he said, is not having anyone with whom to share what I've been reading on the subject, I'm getting really isolated; it happens to everyone, I said. Sometimes I see the layout of the book quite clearly and get enthusiastic, but the odd thing is, the euphoria's almost more difficult to handle on my own than the nausea. And then he went straight on to Sartre. Did I like *Nausea*?

"Well, I don't know, it's a bit overwhelming. It's all so inescapable and, most of all, so serious. I need a breath of humour in novels."

Humourless? How so? He, on the other hand, declared himself a brother to Antoine de Roquentin, and also to Haller, the protagonist of *Steppenwolf*, they were his favourite literary models, he envied them, especially their ability to do without their families, what a cross to bear, he was paying for one of his little brothers to go into a rehab clinic for drug addicts, and the worst thing was that he understood why his brother had got messed up with drugs, of course he understood, if he managed to write the book he was going to dedicate it to his brother, precisely because it was that kind of confusion and desperation, leading down dead end streets, that he wanted to address. He felt closer to his brother than to his parents, the two of them were enclosed in a sort of bunker, united only by their tendency to be scandalised by everything and by the horror that something might spatter them, those inclinations and money were the only things they had in common because they didn't love each other at all, they hated each other without knowing it, between yawns and acid tongues, but it wasn't their fault, deep down he pitied them too. And then, what was going on with young people, did I know?

I shook my head. At the back, against the wall, Vivien Leigh and Clark Gable were kissing in a scene from *Gone with the Wind*. Moisés had just turned 42 and he felt very old, he missed the light, fleeting though it may be, of an extraordinary moment, like the ones Anny, Antoine de Roquentin's girlfriend in *Nausea*, dreamed of, he sighed, his voice faded gradually.

"Yeah. The extraordinary moment. That's what we all miss," I said.

But I didn't feel burdened. There was a redeeming silence, filled with gaseous bodies asking to be embraced. Moisés apologised for going on, but it's just that it had been so long, he said, since anyone had listened to him so attentively; he asked me if I felt like a daiquiri now and I said yes.

"How about you telling me something now?" he asked, when he brought it over.

"A story of extraordinary moments?"

"I wish! If you happened to have one . . ."

Before I realised it, I was taking slow sips of my daiquiri and talking, also in slow sips, about my mother, about one time when the two of us were in a motorboat with some friends and the sea got rough. We were in a lot of danger that afternoon, waves like mountains and her on her feet, keeping everyone's spirits up; the sun was going down and from every spray of foam a little rainbow shot out, as if the colours were being dredged up from the heart of the sea, and fear turned to ecstasy. What I didn't tell Moisés was that I'd been twelve years old, I told him as if it were a recent trip, last summer at most, with my hair as it was tonight, wearing the same dress, I heard my cheerful, clear voice describing those reefs the boat was about to smash against, and she and I were reborn, jarred by the same squall, laughing together, timeless, at the edge of death; and then the hurricane swept away her hat. An example of an extraordinary moment don't you think?

Moisés's eyes had gradually filled with light and I knew, like a drunk finishing a drink after which they know they won't be able to stop, that what I really craved was lying.

"You make me envious," he said. "I never got on well with my parents. How old is your mother?"

"Two months and a few days. That's how long she's been dead."

Moisés's expression darkened as if he'd reached the doom-laden end of a novel. I lowered my gaze to the table and suggestive little lights began to flicker around my glass. Blues, reds, greens. I had to follow the trail of the narrative that had just occurred to me in order to stoke the craving in those eyes in which disappointment was beginning to show, eyes that seemed to be asking for something more, another chapter. I'd brew up a strong drink, why not dare myself? Moisés and I hardly knew each other and he wasn't going to start investigating the truth of the matter, he was simply anxious for an extraordinary tale. It would be a glorious way to leave behind a day that had been so bland, so lacking in passion and secrets. I looked at him. He was upset.

"I'm so sorry!" he said. "You must be going through a terrible time."

I drank the last drops of my daiquiri and made up my mind.

"But not only that . . ." I said, ". . . no, never mind."

His hands crept delicately and decisively over to cover mine. Footsteps passed outside in the street, then faded. Moisés held his breath.

"Not only what?" he asked in a whisper.

"Promise me you won't tell anyone. Just between you and me."

"I swear."

"Well . . . we don't know how she died. That's the worst thing."

"Really?"

The word *really* floated like a frayed little cloud above the bottles lined up on the other side of the bar, made haloes round the heads of Clark Gable and Vivien Leigh, then snaked along the ceiling; the place itself was no longer real.

"What do you mean?" Moisés insisted, considering my silence.

"I don't know, I'm in a daze. So far, it's just a suspicion. The police have opened an investigation. I shouldn't have said anything, don't spread it around, for God's sake."

I stood up in alarm. I had to stop. He believed me. But the glow in Moisés's eyes paid me back with interest. I said sorry and asked him please not to ask me any more questions. I had to go, I didn't feel well. He walked me to my car, silent and fascinated, barely touching my elbow with his hand as we crossed the street. If he had a craving for secrets, I'd given him a large dose. But I also realised that I'd just locked myself out of the Residuo for a good long time, if not forever.

"Please, forget what I told you," I said to him through the car window.

"Don't worry about that. You take care. Are you sure you're all right to drive?"

"I'm sure. Thanks so much for the company. Oh God, where's my head? I haven't even paid you."

He motioned for me to stop rummaging in my handbag.

"Leave it, pay me tomorrow. Come back tomorrow, OK?"

I leaned my head out to kiss him goodbye without promising anything.

On the way home I took a long, unplanned detour. It was very late and the streets were almost deserted and had just been cleaned. I drove through a few red lights stepping hard on the accelerator, shivering with pleasure. A few wisps of fresh air came in the window, messing up my hair.

There was a moment when I was assailed by the temptation to head towards my mother's neighbourhood and drive slowly past her house. Maybe the lights on the fifth floor would be on and I would glimpse suspicious shapes inside. I'd watch from the alley across the street with my headlights turned off. I reacted against the urge almost at once, turning abruptly in the opposite direction. My hands were trembling slightly.

"Can it be?" I said to myself. "I'm as crazy as him, it's contagious. I'm going to end up like Vidal y Villalba!"

VIII

A Cat Who Listens

I spent quite a long time dithering about whether to phone first or just show up, and I think the second option – less compromising by virtue of being more absurd – must have imposed itself on me unexpectedly and without my noticing it, because until I reached the outskirts of Madrid and was heading for Moncloa, I didn't remember where I was going. A taxi driver was honking his horn to tell me my right-hand door wasn't closed properly. I pulled it shut, thanked him with a wave, and that's when I saw, on top of the glove compartment, the little yellow note saying "Visit Dad" attached to a map he'd drawn for me of how to get to the housing development on the other side of Las Rozas where they'd only just moved at the end of April when Mum died. It wasn't a weekend house, he'd explained then, but a real move, Montse couldn't stand the noise of Madrid. "But you'll spend all day on the motorway, won't you?" He shrugged. "Nothing's perfect, dear, we all know that, but it's got its advantages," he'd said, with a smile that, in retrospect, oozed weariness, resignation and incipient old age.

I got lost and arrived late. Not because I lack a sense of direction but because I was in a bit of a stupor. That very morning, when I got back from the Residuo, I'd started writing in the notebook about Vidal y Villalba and realised that I was entering a phase – I didn't know whether long or short – in which my insomnia had overcome the steep slope of painful mysteries and would now begin down the florid path of pleasurable ones.

When dawn broke, it was so bright that I decided to clear out the kitchen, the coolest part of the house, clean it thoroughly and set up a provisional office there. I brought in an adjustable table lamp, which replaced the electric mixer, and dragged the big table up to the window. It had never occurred to me to write there, it seemed like a miracle to see it cleared of kitchen gadgets, transformed with books and folders, to have created a space so much my own on top of someone else's geography, which had always exuded tedium and imposed itself on me as alien. Inventing this new possibility for it was like caressing a neglected patient and eliciting a smile.

I wandered through the other rooms collecting the things I needed, making sure they formed a harmonious group: books, paperweights, card index, clock, a little tray for my pencils, and even a rosebud – cut from the balcony – in a small vase. Gerundio, the grey tabby striped with white and cinnamon, followed my steps, miaowing and rubbing up against my legs. I gave him a bowl of milk, which he drank licking his whiskers, then he leapt on to the table and settled down on top of a *History of the Reign of Carlos III* with such elegance that I hadn't the heart to tell him to scat. He looked like a totem. The whole soul of that room, so recently inhospitable, expanded and came back to life.

I opened the notebook and sat down. First, as a prelude, a mention of Tupac Amaru. For a while I sat still, breathing slowly, with my elbows on the table, forehead resting on my hands and eyes closed, as if at prayer. I wasn't the slightest bit tired, but I did have that fluttering feeling of unreality that precedes surprises; every once in a while I half-opened my eyes and the lamplight sliding over Gerundio's velvety back seemed to be sending coded warnings that found an echo in his soft purring, which was more human than feline. Until at last I realised I needed to talk to him before I started to write, that he'd got up there to listen to me and if I told him the story of Tupac Amaru as if to a fairy-tale cat, not only would he understand but he might help me to understand it better by contributing some secret piece of information. I raised my eyes and we looked at one another.

"OK," I said. "Request granted. Right away, but wait, let's see, where to begin . . ."

I spread the papers and cards that contained the choicest quotes about that preliminary story around me in a semi-circle between my notebook and the pedestal of books on which he was perched. He watched me arrange that almost necromantic pack of cards with his wise green eyes half-closed.

"You see, Gerundio . . . Spain conquered America, which was an immense country full of Indians – they wandered freely with their own rituals and dances and customs – Columbus arrived in the caravels and made them toe the line, in accordance with the will of the Catholic Monarchs, anyway, you already know that, it's in the encyclopaedias and I don't want to be too long-winded. Two centuries go by, and the zeal to enslave the Indians and make them obedient subjects of the King of Spain increases as more countries and more gold mines are discovered, they can't govern them from far away so they send over military officers, viceroys and firm-handed administrators who don't get on very well with the natives, impossible, it's as if I decided to cut off your tail and make you less of a cat, a wealth of problems arise. Now we're up to the reign of Carlos III, a period of history, by the way, that you're sitting on top of and I may have to ask you to move to look something up, but not yet, you stay there, I see you're following my drift, while I, on the other hand, am getting rather confused."

I noticed something very surprising. Each time I stopped speaking, Gerundio's purring, hushed by my words, would start up again, sounding steadily more wheedling, like the protest of a child who thinks people are about to stop paying attention to him. It's not quite crying. I don't think a word exists to describe it, there's something of an erotic moan to it. It sounds like a trapped "u" trying to escape through the nose. Suddenly I remembered that my mother called it "ninfring", one of the many words she invented, I used to make that noise as a little girl when she'd come in to tell me stories at night, if she stopped in the middle of one, maybe to see if I was asleep yet. Here was a first secret piece of information, a little lost stone unearthed. I stroked the cat's tail.

"Don't ninfrie, Gerundio. I was just thinking. Maybe it's not good to think too much when you're telling a story, but so many things happen in this one. Hang on, I need to draw something for you."

I began to draw a map of America and the outline of Spain above it and to the right, so he could see how far apart they were, how much sea the ships had to ply so that news and merchandise from the colonies could reach Carlos III, the affable and pious Monarch, who was most often to be found hunting stags in the Pardo. I've always enjoyed drawing maps, it gives me a special pleasure, history can't be understood without geography, I was glad I'd put a few coloured pencils in the little tray; around the coasts the blue of the sea had the intensity of a halo.

"You see now, Gerundio, how far Madrid is from Peru? It was a ceaseless toing and froing, ships and more ships, but the Spaniards were all in it for themselves, to make a fortune, and taking advantage of the Indians didn't trouble anyone, they thought of them as a bunch of savages dressed in feathers, and so unrest spread, because the Indians couldn't bear so many taxes and punishments any more. The blame lay with the magistrates known as *corregidores* – individuals acting as both 'merchants and judges who perverted justice by entangling it with commerce' – as well as with the customs officials. Some Indian children in Arequipa actually killed one of their playmates who had willingly taken on the rôle of a customs official, that's how bad things were getting, I'm talking about 1770, I don't know where you might have been at that time, Gerundio, or what you might have been.

"OK, let's go to Peru, that's this big province I've coloured yellow with brown shadows in the middle that represent the cordillera of the Andes. This is where the first outbursts of rebellion began, because the Indians, as one report puts it, 'weren't allowed the breath to complain', but complaints can be written down, well-argued pasquinades flew around, in which the ancient paternal government of the Inca kings was praised, in contrast to the despotism of the *corregidores*. Between Tucumán and Cuzco, just here, a handsome young mule-driver, descended from princes, propagated insurrection by throwing pamphlets in the air. You like how things are going, don't you? His name was Tupac Amaru, which means, 'resplendent serpent'."

The slow and solemn snaking of Gerundio's tail as he heard those words took me by surprise. I didn't dare look him in the eye. But the sudden suspicion that he might already know the whole story didn't prevent me from continuing. On the contrary, it added emotion to my tale.

"José Gabriel Tupac Amaru, a descendent of the ancient dynasties of Peru, who had attended the University of Lima, became the ringleader of a war, which began on 4 November 1780, when he threw a rope around the neck of Corregidor Arriaga, as he came riding in on a mule, and ordered that the official be hanged. Tupac Amaru immediately recruited people, took to the hills, and set up camp on steep heights beside gorges and rivers that were difficult to ford. Here it says what he was like, I'll read it to you:

> "He always rode a white horse and wore a blue velvet suit trimmed with gold, and over it a shirt or Indian's *unco*, a scarlet cape, a tricorn hat, a gold braid tied around his

forehead as an emblem of the dignity of his ancestors and a chain of the same metal around his neck with a pendant in the shape of the sun. His weapons: two blunderbusses, pistols and a sword; from the crowds he received constant signs of enthusiasm and reverence.

"The war didn't last long, Gerundio, six months, it was very cruel and the Spaniards won, although not as easily as they'd expected to, that's why after it was over they were so afraid of the Indians and those who'd supported them. They sent six columns with 15,000 soldiers under the command of a certain Don José del Valle, but Tupac Amaru escaped from his grasp again and again.

"When they finally caught him, they executed him in the plaza at Cuzco along with his wife, Micaela Bastida, his 20-year-old son Hipólito and countless relatives and friends. It was 18 May 1781, I'll read you a witness's account, although it's very sad, I think so, anyway, it makes my heart recoil:

"The spectacle was concluded with the rebel José Gabriel who was brought to the middle of the square, and there the executioner cut out his tongue. They took off his chains and laid him down on the ground. They tied four ropes to his hands and feet and attached the ropes to the girths of four horses, which four mestizos drove in four different directions. Cuzco had never before seen a spectacle of this kind. Either because the horses were not very strong or because the Indian was really made of iron, they simply could not tear him apart, although they tugged at him for a long time, while he dangled in the air like a spider."

In one agile leap, practically flying, Gerundio flung himself on to my lap from his pedestal of books, curled up in a ball and started miaowing pitifully. Bent over him, I kissed his ears and scratched his neck, almost with tears in my eyes.

"Poor Tupac," I murmured. "Thank goodness for reincarnation."

I turned off the lamp because daylight was streaming in and Gerundio escaped on to the balcony. He was back to his old self, the stray cat who'd slipped into our house last summer leaping from roof to roof with a broken leg.

I pulled the blinds down a little and made myself coffee. I was shocked at the extremely different rhythms time can take on from one moment to the next, depending on our willingness to collaborate with it.

At 9.30 I telephoned the Archive and asked for Magda, a colleague who's very fond of me, so much so that I sometimes find her rather oppressive. In fact, she's my boss. I put on an ill voice, which sounded very convincing. I couldn't come in. I'd had a very restless night, chills and fever. Now my head was pounding and my throat was agony.

"I'm not surprised," she said, "it's from sweating so much. Have you got air-conditioning?"

"Yes."

"Say no more, it's the bane of humanity. You should take your temperature."

"I already have. It's 39.5."

"That's really high. Take a Clamoxil right away. Have you got someone to look after you? Because if you don't, I could come over this afternoon and bring you whatever you need."

"Thanks, but don't worry. My mother-in-law's here."

That was my last lie before I started to unravel those of Vidal y Villalba, or perhaps to simply put them down one after the other and see whether I could devise a trail of little stones that would lead me to reconstruct his unsuccessful schemer's paranoia.

The most important thing about that sleepless night is that in telling the tale to Gerundio, I had opened the way to the written word. I lost my fear of Tomás's notebook and it was like unblocking a drain. I began decisively, unafraid of crossing things out or repeating myself. It was a draft. Well then, so what? The thing was to set down more or less formless things about a man who was a liar but not my own invention, pay attention here, someone who had actually lived, and our lives are always in drafts, just as we suffer them, there's never time to produce a final version. The advantage was that he didn't have his teeth in me, I could even embellish the story with an explanation as to why I'd become interested in it, I wasn't obliged to lie.

For Ambroise Dupont, who made me a gift of a paper flower, I wrote on the first page.

IX

Standstill in Las Rozas

Although I hadn't slept a wink for more than 30 hours, my reflexes were functioning well, but once I'd passed the exits for El Plantío and Majadahonda, I was forced to call on all my reserves of good sense in order to quell the intense suspicion that I was experiencing a hallucination. I was getting close to Las Rozas and the billboards for Leroy Merlin Construction Materials, Európolis and Campsa were making me dizzy by treacherously superimposing themselves over another picture which would have had the same setting: that team of cavalry escorting a prisoner, who claimed to be called Luis Vidal y Villalba, and whom I'd just left raving, his feet shackled, in my kitchen.

I left the main road and went into the town of Las Rozas, although my father's map made it very clear that this was not the advisable way to the housing development. More than that, he'd drawn – one beside the other and separated by a line – two different routes, each with its little arrows and crosses, and the one I'd taken, titled in his handwriting as "Option no. 1", was crossed out with a red X, I remembered the fat marker he took out and how he then exchanged it for a pen and wrote underneath: "Misleading trail". I didn't recognise the words then, nor did I make any effort to, I was hardly capable of effort at that moment, nothing mattered, but I liked it that he'd ignored other demands on him in order to pay attention to me. He'd taken me aside at the cemetery gates, avoiding the mess of cars trying to pull out, I'd just asked him please not to call me for a while, told him that I needed to be alone. "I really will come and see you, Dad, when you're least expecting it, you know me. But not right away." We looked at each other through our respective sunglasses, and there was a lot of truth in that smudge of shared light that isolated us from the sweep of footsteps and voices, from the intense scent of flowers condemned to die. His reply was to take me by the shoulders and separate us from the crowd. "If I don't explain to you exactly where we live, it'll be more of an uphill struggle to make the indecision," he said, smiling. "It's not easy to find, you know? If I'm a bit distracted, I still go the wrong way, I'll put the phone number down too, but show up without warning if you want, you've always been one for spur-of-the-moment impulses." He sat down on a bench and I stood in front of him, watching him take a pad of paper out of his coat pocket and rest it on his knee, moved that he carried a pad of paper and a red marker around with him and that he should mention the two poles around which the skein of my days are wound: impetuosity and indecision. My somnolent eyes looked over the bits of grey that have intermingled in his hair for a few years now, at his fingers, agile as ever, and at those strange lines he was drawing, without hurrying, to help me find a particular route (he must have noticed I was wandering without a compass), a bridge or, who knows, perhaps a tunnel, it didn't matter, those hieroglyphics lead away from stasis and into adventure if you can only work them out. He was inventing a new one for me now; when I was little we both liked the puzzles in the newspaper and I'd complain they were too easy, I remember the smell of the Sunday paper, how I wanted to meet the people whose photos appeared in its pages, to be grown-up, to go travelling without a destination, I loved movies about hitch-hiking kids who spent their lives on the road. Dad works in an advertising design company, he makes a lot of money now, but when he and Mum got engaged both of them wanted to become famous painters, she persevered, he worked as an architectural draughtsman for a time, these are anecdotes that belong to prehistory. With my arrival in the world it seems that their dreams of the bohemian life ended, and an anxious noise started, the kind of noise that strengthens quarrels behind closed doors, quarrels whose poisonous gas slips out through the gap; illogical arguments, thrown down the slope of my memory, an archive where no-one's ever tried to put things in order. But when Dad starts drawing – I thought that day – it all fades away like a bad dream, and no-one's old or will see threatening teeth bared in the morning, instead a lazy music plays, we've all three slept in and there's the smell of coffee, it's Sunday.

I could have told him that I almost never do anything on "the spur of the moment" any more, sat down on that bench and thrown my arms around his neck and cried for everything that got mixed up, broken, incomprehensible, for all those unsolved puzzles. But I didn't move or take my hands out of my pockets, I remember the feel of my key ring, a medal of St Christopher. Then he stood up, gave me a hug and handed me the paper, urging me not to lose it. "Don't worry, I won't." Montse was already demanding his company from a distance, made anxious by not being able to find him for a few seconds. "Ismael, please, Ismael." Not even at a funeral could she keep herself discreetly in the shadows; and now she was approaching with tiny steps as I took the piece of notepaper, folded it calmly, and that deep sea between my father and me darkened, penned in by the black parentheses of our glasses, more unfathomable the longer we took to say goodbye, like a secret, disturbing wood whose dangers united us and which Montse could never go down to or even peek at, no matter how much she waved her hand and raised her voice in an attempt to draw our attention to some trivial problem to do with a car that would be blocking others if they didn't move it soon. Dad took one indecisive step in that direction, what car?

She said, "The Volvo, Ismael, our Volvo," and it sounded like an obscenity on her lips, which were painted a very dark carmine. Behind her, as if in slow motion, came other groups of people, possibly not all from our ceremony, there are people who filter in from other stories – just as Vidal y Villalba's is melded with the bishop of Mondoñedo's – they stray in, look around and before asking anything burst into tears on a mistaken shoulder unsure whether to shake off the intruder or accept him as a comrade in universal bereavement. After all, what those absent – whether by virtue of leukaemia, old age, a car accident, cancer or stabbing – all have in common is that they're conspicuous by their absence and leave a similar orphanhood, the same trace of bewilderment.

An impression of trepidation always reigns at funerals, the sensation of prowling around quicksand, and the worrying thing is that no-one knows who's organising the expedition or laying down the guidelines; the living have never studied each other so closely, as if hoping to discover which of them might look like a possible captain. Any false step can set us spiralling towards an unforeseen destiny.

I found it very sad to fold the bit of notepaper, put it away and articulate a "Thanks, Dad, bye" that revealed no emotion whatsoever, instead of kissing him beside his ear and whispering: "Don't go, please, leave Montse, don't pay any attention, don't let her snatch you away, what's Montse doing here anyway, let's go have a coffee right now, we'll speed off, if I run away, will you follow me?" But all I said was thanks and goodbye.

I've spent half my life telling my parents things that have no connection to what I really want to say to them, honing my voice to adapt to a betrayal that gradually stopped being one as I ceded to the pacts of concealment and half-truths that their relationship seemed to suggest as an unconscious palliative, alleviating concern without delving into its causes. I learned from quite an early age to look at myself in that oblique mirror from which my face peered back at me half-obscured by theirs, but I didn't realise that the smiles were crooked until the mirror began to reflect Mum and me on our own, with the shadow of him in the background. I tried to erase that shadow, I rubbed it out furiously again and again, but it would reappear like the bloodstain on Bluebeard's key, and in the mirror gestures froze, nothing was real, all the chairs were missing a leg, there was no breeze, there were ashes on the shelves instead of books, my face was blue and our bodies tilted as if they were about to keel over, like those dolls that don't sit up properly. Wasn't it simply that some people – I began to think – had married the wrong person, and we'd all be better off each to her own, as she used to say, conquering our own portion of air? Mum would stand looking out the window as she dropped this suggestion, stained with the colours from her brushes – bilious yellow, pearly white or garnet – and my heart would contract before her sharp, impatient birdlike profile. "Don't go," I'd think, "don't fly away." Then everything would return to how it had been before, although the threat could reappear at any time, and I knew it. But it was so difficult to seek out your own portion of air, endure the open air once you'd developed a taste for half-measures, abandon the cave without bitterness or injury, resign yourself to forgetting what you'd never understood.

Anyway, I came to understand – though at some cost – the extent to which my image had become distorted within a quicksilver made murky by dark family vices, vices I inherited blindly, blameless and unhappy. And one day I said: Enough! And I broke that mirror. But I broke it badly, because its shards still cling to me. I didn't know how to sweep them away. My spur-of-the moment impulses have never been much use. That must have been what I felt like talking to Dad about. Although I knew I wasn't going to.

I parked in the first little plaza where I saw a space, got out for a breath of fresh air. The breeze was starting to pick up and it was less stifling than the day before. I sat at a table on the terrace of a bar, ordered a beer and took the piece of paper out of my handbag. Underneath the route crossed out with a red X he'd written: "Misleading trail. That way you'll get lost for sure." Well, I sighed, I'd gone down the misleading trail, it's not an unknown situation for me and it has its attractions because it leads to reflection. In children's games, in fairy tales, in guessing games, there's always at least one misleading trail. They're also found in detective fiction, in legal investigations and in conjectures over lovers' suspicious behaviour. Setting truth against deception is the perfect game, although a difficult one: either we deceive or we are deceived.

There can be several simultaneous matches played on the same board, we never pay attention to just one of them, though it might seem that we do. For example, if I continued my inquiries into an 18th-century adventurer and his lies, was it not in order to slip away from the weight of another pressing and much more devious investigation which interfered with it? That's why I'd got lost and had to stop to recapitulate; a knot, a crossroads, at a standstill in Las Rozas.

The beer was nice and cold and I felt good. I ordered another. Las Rozas isn't a town any more, but a district annexed to Madrid, and if there were ever any 18th-century buildings, there aren't any left. I looked around: cafés, a supermarket, a yellow letter box, a mixed-race couple, boys on motorbikes, a lady with her dog, badly parked cars, just like any neighbourhood. It was all a mirage, not even as a theatre set could it help me evoke the arrival of a cavalry team escorting a prisoner who's anxiously awaited at Court, suspected of being very dangerous, of conspiring in London with rebel Jesuits, of perhaps having known Tupac Amaru and his followers, he must be tortured so he'll confess, poor Don Luis. Carlos III's ministers did not know the truth I was starting to perceive, and which made me feel sorry for him, nor could they ever drag it out of that prisoner, incapable of travelling any paths other than illusory ones, and, by the time he arrived at Las Rozas, already ensnared in a tangle of delusions. He might not have allowed me to approach and tear off his conspirator's mask. He would have felt that to be more humiliating than prison itself.

I paid for the second beer and stood up, in a very agreeable state of laxity, filled with an urge to say or do something outrageous. Because it was all so unimportant . . .

As I made my way across the little plaza towards my car, it occurred to me, just like that, to ask two middle-aged women who had stopped in front of a shop window if they knew Don Vidal y Villalba. One shrugged her shoulders but the other said:

"You mean Vidal y Varela."

"Well, I don't know. I might have it mixed up."

"Who?" the other wanted to know.

"You know, the new orthodontist who's moved into the street across the way, Number Five. I'm not sure, but the office may have closed by now."

"Is he a dentist, the man you're looking for?" the other one asked, perhaps surprised by my silence.

"It's possible, he used to be in prison. You know how it is, Señora, the world never stops spinning and we all make mistakes. Thanks anyway."

I got in the car with a smile and they stared at me as if I was a complete lunatic. But how funny. Wandering around there was a sort of double of the 18th-century prisoner, whose surname, I had to admit, was more suited to a dentist than to a conspirator. In any case, my teeth are in good shape. I put on some music before I drove away.

X

Visit to the Indian Settlement

I arrived late at the housing development where my father lived, after going round in a thousand circles. I say late because the sun had set, not because anyone was expecting me. Some of the verandas were lit up and through open doors came the shifting, tinted glow of televisions. Almost all the side streets, recently laid out, were half-built and there were cranes in abundance. There was no-one to be seen.

I'd slowed down, and as I ploughed through the central avenue, letting my gaze slide over gardens and fences in search of the number 73 or a letter box with my own surname on it, I began to feel the same kind of strangeness that you see in the faces of certain travellers in westerns. They've just got off a train. They don't know the lie of the land either, and from something said earlier you can assume they're following someone's trail or a forgotten story with confusing clues. And they stop, disoriented, with an air of defencelessness. What have they come here for? Wouldn't it be better to forget it?

A removal van had stopped almost at the end of the avenue and two big men were unloading a piano. A huge dog with a studded collar was barking furiously with its paws up on the iron gate of the house towards which the hauliers were carrying the piano. They put it down, conferred, and said something to the driver, who stuck his head and then a hand out, gesturing from the cab window. At this moment a blond-haired boy of about eight came running out of the house and started shouting at the dog and pulling him back. It was my brother Esteban. I stopped the car and got out.

As I went closer, the dog seemed bigger and his teeth sharper. It seemed impressive that such a skinny little boy would dare to drag him by the collar or try to convince him of anything.

"Down, Fiero! Here, Fiero!" he scolded. "Mummy, come out, the piano's here!"

"And so fierce!" said one of the men. "Man, the deterrents these people spend their money on! Hey kid, why don't you tie him up?"

"He doesn't do anything. He's just trying to scare you. Mum! Once he knows you he won't do anything. Right, Fiero?"

"That's a relief," the other man remarked. "Well, tell him my name's Juan, or do we have to show him our ID?"

"Martínez Transport Company might make him take us more seriously!" the driver shouted from the cab, with a noticeable backstreet Madrid accent. "On you go, boys, I think we've won him over!"

The barking was abating in fact, and so the two men picked up the piano again, laughing. It was made of dark wood and wasn't too big. I stayed half-hidden behind the truck.

Montse, in jeans and a low-cut shirt, had just appeared on the veranda, and after turning on the outside lights, some of which shone up from the lawn, took the dog to chain him up to a ring. Then she returned to take charge of the piano's expedition across the garden, urging the hauliers to be careful in an authoritarian voice and advising them of the unevenness of the ground, of cables, mounds of earth and steps on which they might trip. She was walking backwards as she did so, lost her balance halfway across the lawn and fell into a flower bed.

Another figure appeared on the veranda, not Dad, but a woman of more or less the same age as Montse, a friend perhaps. She had a boyish haircut and wore a miniskirt.

"Are you OK?" she asked in a shrill voice.

Montse had already got up and was brushing off her jeans.

"Damn cables!" she said angrily. "It was nothing. Tell Gregoria to open the back doors, we're going to take the piano in through the kitchen."

"I'm going too!" said Esteban. "Wait for me, Aunt Loli!"

He ran up to the veranda and disappeared inside the house, following the girl in the miniskirt. It was a two-storeyed villa, quite pretentious and flashy. With it, for the moment, the housing development ended. Beyond was just a clearing and an attempt at a street. I came out of my hiding place, sneaked past the gate and round that side of the house. I've always loved spying on people and getting a different perspective. It was pretty unlikely that Montse would see me, so absorbed was she in her task, but there was still some danger. I crouched down a little.

The garden was very large, much bigger than those of the other houses, and it was decorated in the "look but don't touch" manner, maybe under the auspices of some landscape designer impressed by *House and Garden*. I imagined Montse pointing at one of those glossy pages ("I want a nook like that one, just like it!") and then arguing with Dad later about the cost. There was a pair of quite horrible statues, wrought-iron benches and a swinging chair with an awning. A grotto made of artificial stone, which didn't really fit in, shot streams of water out of some sort of shell into the kidney-shaped pool. It bore no relation to the pond of greenish water I'd seen in my dream, and that black hole vomiting filth was nowhere to be seen either, despite my painstaking, almost anxious, search for it, as one does when a fundamental reason for something slips through one's fingers or out of one's memory. "I expect that's what would have made sense of my visit," I thought, "now I know why I came here: to find the black hole and explore it."

I stood unseen regarding the entire scene through the iron

fence railings until the cortège rounded the corner and the outside lights were turned off. I guessed that it would be a while before anyone came back out, so I made a move and, taking advantage of the open gate, went cautiously into the garden. I looked behind me. The driver wasn't in the van any more. I advanced, careful not to trip over any cables, and sank into the extremely soft cushions of the garden swing. The first star had begun to blink in the pale sky, I took a deep breath and started swinging. What pleasure! No-one would imagine I was there. "I've entered a fairy tale," I thought. I felt tired, but so free and detached from everything, like when you put down a heavy piece of luggage after carrying it around for hours. How long had it been since I'd slept? I began to add up the hours and felt my eyes close as I did so. Don Luis Vidal y Villalba, in a white dentist's coat, was dissolving among distant clouds, he wanted to tell me something, but when he opened his mouth no sound came out, then he turned into a whorl of smoke.

I was brought back to reality by a barking that soon stopped, the sputter of a motor starting up and the sense that someone was nearby. I opened my eyes. Esteban stood in front of me, staring as if at an apparition. Night had fallen and the removal van was driving away. I sat up. I'd almost been lying on the cushions, and felt a tingling in one of my legs that had been bent at an odd angle. I rubbed it.

"Why did you fall asleep on the swing?" Esteban asked. "It's not yours. This isn't your house. Who are you?"

"I'm your sister."

"Liar. You're too old. And you're not blonde. The one in the photo is blonde."

"Hair darkens with age."

He thought for a minute. "Or you can dye it. My mum dyes hers. She gives it highlights."

"Well, I don't."

I bent over to retrieve a shoe that had slipped off. From inside the house came angry voices. Neither of them was Dad's.

"But you're silly," said Esteban. "And a liar."

"Liar, liar / silly thing, / butterfly-er / look, on the wing."

I stood up and started to flap my arms as if they were wings. The verse just came out to the tune of a skipping rhyme. When I used to do inter-rock, the lyrics always came to me like that, almost without a thought, the music gave me more trouble. Esteban was fascinated. He took a moment to react.

"And that song?"

"I just made it up."

"Truly?"

"Truly, no, because I'm a liar. Hadn't we agreed on that?"

He smiled at me for the first time. "Well, make up another one, come on. About watches."

"Watches? I can't think of one about watches. 'Watch' only rhymes with 'botch'. That reminds me, what time is it? I forgot my watch, that was a botch, oh, little brother, my heart's all a-flutter, I'm going to be late, with sleep I've got a date, so I'm off out the gate."

"Wow, it just comes to you, that's cool. Why don't we make up a verse, half-each? You're not really going, are you?"

"I think so, because I'm really tired. I've come from London to Las Rozas and now they want to put me in jail. Your father's not home, by any chance, is he?"

He started hopping in circles and sticking his tongue out at me.

"You want him to protect you from the police?"

"That's it exactly. You're a clever one."

"Well, he's not home, but Mum and Aunt Loli are."

"They're no use to me. I doubt they'd want to get involved in anything to do with police, what do you think?"

Voices raised in argument were still coming from the villa. Now the lights were on upstairs.

"No," said Esteban. "Mum's really mad, 'cos, they brought the piano, you know?"

"Yeah. I came in the cab of the removal van, that's how I know, I showed them the way here."

"Liar! The driver was fat."

"Well, they're not going to put me in jail, either. We'd decided I lied, no?"

He shrugged his shoulders sulkily.

"Answer, yes or no?"

"You're bossy! Yes! But I'm only answering because I want to, not because you told me to. What are you laughing at?"

"When I was little I used to say the very same thing. Come on, I won't lie any more, don't get stroppy. Why's your mother angry? Because I'm here?"

"Nah! She hasn't even seen you. Because they scratched the piano a bit taking it in and because Dad's not home yet. She wants him to be really excited about the piano."

"Are you going to play it?"

"Nope, I'm going to be a drummer. She played it when she was little in my grandparents' village, villancicos, tangos and 'For Elise', they've had it there till now because it wouldn't fit in the old house. It was smaller than this one, but I liked it better because Manolito and Lauri were there."

Inside the villa the aggression in the women's voices was rising.

"Mind your own business! Got it?" Montse's shouting could be heard clearly from the garden.

"So, don't call me, and that'll be that! As if it were my idea of fun coming out here! I've had it up to here with you, I swear!" said the other voice. "I'm leaving."

"But she won't leave," Esteban explained, looking towards the house. "They're always the same. It's about the piano, they don't know where to put it. And because Aunt Loli says we'll see if Mum has the patience to practise every day, and learn something a little more modern, Aunt Loli is very modern, she laughs and Mum gets a bit nervous. It's 'cos she's slimming, you know? Now Gregoria never makes puddings so she won't get jealous. Hey, you don't have any sweets, do you?"

"No sweets. Chewing gum, maybe. Hang on, let me see."

"I like gum too."

He came close and peered into my handbag as I rifled through it. I gave him a piece of gum, which came out stuck to a broken necklace, Tomás says my handbags resemble a conjurer's bag of tricks.

"Here, it's strawberry."

He peeled off the silver paper and stuck the gum in his mouth.

"Nothing else?" he asked as he chewed. "Haven't you brought me any other presents? What a sister!"

By way of an answer, I emptied the contents of my bag on the cushions of the swing. I spotted a little calculator I'd never actually used. It was gold, in the shape of a powder compact. One of those stupid impulse buys made in a big department store on a depressed afternoon. I showed it to Esteban and he studied it carefully.

"What do you think?"

"Well, I have one already but it's not as cool. Will you give it to me?"

"OK."

I watched him open it, press the little buttons and start to use it with total ease. Soon he got bored, stuck it in his pocket and started running in circles around me as I put the things back in my bag.

"But what I like best," he said, "is when you make up rhymes."

At that moment a voice bellowed from the bottom of the garden.

"Esteban! Where'd you get to? Come and have dinner!"

"That's Gregoria," he said. "I'm going to tell Mum you're here, OK?"

And he ran off towards the house. I waited till I saw him disappear into the veranda and escaped furtively, in the shadow of the garden wall, and walked to my car. I couldn't understand why I felt like crying.

The meandering return journey through streets, un-signposted roundabouts and dark fields lightened my melancholy through its repetition – going round in circles again, always the same, lost, not knowing why I do what I do, making indecisions, what a nightmare. When will I wake up? "When the city is a murmur of ashes roasting down below and all the streams flow clean." Who said that inside my head? I didn't remember it as the fragment of any poem I knew but I liked it, so I pulled over, turned on my indicators and wrote it down in the diary I pulled out of my conjurer's bag, in a section I call "EXCRESCENCES". Outside it was very dark, no-one drove past, there were just a few lonely buildings and I felt afraid. "It always happens at the end of nightmares, it means you're about to wake up," I told myself in order to calm down.

So when I noticed a girl get out of a car on the pavement across the road and wave goodbye to someone who stayed behind the steering wheel waiting to see her safely inside, I honked the horn a couple of times and leaned out the window.

"Excuse me, please! Excuse me!"

The driver turned his head. So he'd heard me, another person had entered my nightmare. He looked at me as if he couldn't believe his eyes, got out of the car and crossed the street.

"What are you doing here?" he asked.

"What do you think, spying on you."

On his face I could read the exhaustion of someone making an effort to find an explanation after having given so many in the course of the day. And he was going to need even more when he got home. I felt sorry for him.

"Well," he said, "I suppose you won't believe it's a girl from work."

He was obviously embarrassed. I started to laugh.

"Dad, for God's sake, I don't believe anything. Do I look like Sherlock Holmes to you? Don't lose your sense of humour. Go and put her mind at ease, go on," I added, my eyes glued to the pavement across the street, "she's looking slightly suspicious. If you don't want to admit to a daughter of my size, tell her I'm lost. Both are true."

"Ok, thanks. But wait."

His submissive voice, and the way he walked to the front door where the girl seemed to be waiting to see what was going on, reminded me of the actions of a little boy in a tight spot obeying the advice of an adult. My hopes, already unlikely, of finding consolation and support in him vanished. But there remained a trace of tenderness for his familiar outline, his voice was the same, his shoulders rose as usual, he walked the same way, his glasses were a little dirty, he had that habit of clenching his jaw, and I still felt protective towards him; I'd known him to be weaker than my mother since I was a child.

I bowed my head towards my hands and again it was as if there was an invisible helm between them. I swallowed. I didn't want to look towards the door, or discover how long he was taking to say goodnight to that girl. I didn't want to smoke either. I wasn't nervous, just really tired, but prepared not to add my fatigue to his own. I was used to it.

When he came back, I greeted him with a smile but didn't invite him to sit beside me, and he seemed relieved. He leaned lightly against the car door.

"So . . . some days are trials," he said, now without subterfuge, like a little boy caught fibbing.

"You said it, chief. Let me clean your glasses, come on, maybe it'll help you see things more clearly."

He was always losing them, although he had two spare pairs, always dirty, sometimes he used to hand them to Mum or to me, wearing a particular expression, "How can I be so useless?" He passed them to me and rubbed his eyes. He must have been remembering. The glasses he had now were frameless and the lenses were thicker.

Bewildered by fatigue, we exchanged a few fragmentary facts about our respective situations through the window, and it became clear – something which seemed to worry him a little – that I had not actually seen Montse. Then he tried to lose himself in flimsy excuses, but that bored me. It was past 11 p.m. I suggested that he save some energy for when he got home, that he was going to need it. With me he was in the clear.

"Don't waste your breath, Dad. You've got a piano waiting for you, along with a miniskirted sister-in-law and Montse's nerves. Look how your glasses have come out. Better?"

"Good work, thanks."

"OK then, *ciao*. I just have to ask you one favour that'll cost you a couple of minutes. Be my guide and get me out to the main road. I'm lost in this Indian settlement."

"Of course. But first, tell me, did you come out here for some specific reason?"

"I don't think so. Perhaps to ask if you still solve difficult crossword puzzles."

He put his hand on my bare arm.

"Not any more. Who am I going to fool? Everything difficult befuddles me these days."

"So, I guess you spend your days being befuddled."

"More or less. And you?"

"Depends on the time, the noise level and the colour of the sky. But crossword puzzles still help me a lot. Especially inventing them."

"I meant are you all right."

"Just fine, Dad, don't worry. We'll talk another time . . . Hey, just one thing, what did Mum die of?"

He looked very surprised. "Of an aneurism. You knew that, didn't you?"

"Yes, but it's such an ugly word. It doesn't suit her, and besides . . ."

"Besides what?"

"I mean did she just suddenly fall down and that was it?"

"Yes, there wasn't even time to call an ambulance, that's what Rosario said, she was with her."

"But there'll be a report, I suppose. Didn't they do an autopsy?"

"Not that I know of," Dad said, taken aback. "What are you worried about?"

"Nothing, it's just that I wasn't in Madrid, you'll remember, and I didn't get back in time to see her alive . . ."

"Of course I remember! But I thought you would have talked to Rosario."

"Well no, it's something I need to do, one of many, she's left me several messages . . . well, quite a few, but I've been a bit lazy about seeing her."

The pressure of his hand on my forearm grew stronger.

"Just lazy?"

"Lazy or whatever. Leave it."

It had come out sounding hasty and cutting. Suddenly I thought of Ramiro, of my scowl reflected in his ironic look; I spend my life on the defensive, unaware of the harm I might cause people, that I cause myself. Dad shrugged his shoulders and took his hand away.

"You said it," he observed, sounding overwhelmed.

I saw red: incipient exasperation.

"I'm sorry, Dad. It's just that I'm incapable of dialling that number. I know it's nonsense and I'll get over it, but I refused to see her once she was dead, and as long as I don't call I'm maintaining the illusion, do you understand? I keep thinking she'll answer, it's the voice that takes the longest to die, it's the soul when all's said and done."

"But remember, sometimes Mum's voice would set your nerves on edge."

"Well, there you go. Now I'd give anything to hear it. I'd be satisfied with five minutes, even if she was just telling me off, which she never did, unfortunately."

I'd lowered my eyes and the pause that followed didn't bother me. No response seemed to be required. I noticed he'd moved closer to me again.

"Look at me," he said unexpectedly.

I did so, and in that look all of the evening's arguments dissolved.

"I'm luckier than you," he said in a serious tone. "I can still hear her voice by listening to you. And see her by looking at you."

I opened the car door, got out, and we hugged each other very tight. There are people who don't smell of anything, and others you recognise by their scent. Dad smelled the same as ever, his scent was indefinable. Trembling a little, he started to kiss my hair. He'd never kissed me like that. He didn't let go. "Now I'm ready to pass the test of talking to Grandfather. Now I am her," I thought. And there was something of a triumph in that admission. I stroked the back of Dad's neck and gently pulled away.

"Come on, Dad, if your neighbour from across the street looks out her window, the tale of the lost motorist is going to sound like a tall story."

"I don't think she's the type to do that," he smiled. "And besides, I don't care."

"Just in case. OK, sheriff, are you going to get me out of this Indian settlement?"

"Sure thing, stranger. Good luck," he said. "When you reach the mountains you'll find a fresh horse waiting for you."

The main road was nearby. He drove there in front of me and waved goodbye before turning back down a curved street that would take him home.

I took the first opportunity to turn around and headed away from Madrid. Going towards El Escorial, I was only a few kilometres from the home in which my grandfather lived. This was another zone of the Indian settlement, perhaps the most remote and dangerous. I was already near the mountains, but I didn't see the fresh horse. When I arrived, almost all the lights were out. I turned off the headlights, without driving right into the squalid yard, and rummaged in my conjurer's bag. I always carried a pad of paper and envelopes, just in case. I wrote two short notes. The first said:

"Esteemed friend, Several days have passed since our conversation. I think I am beginning to feel ready for the game you suggested, or perhaps we should call it an experiment. As a prelude, and taking advantage of the fact that my handwriting (not only my voice) resembles my mother's, could you give the enclosed letter to my grandfather Basilio, if you think it appropriate. It is in an unsealed envelope so you can read it and judge for yourself. I await your call. Sincerely, A.S.L."

"Dear Papa," read the text of the other, "Forgive me for taking so long to get in touch with you, but I've been in a country where the post doesn't function very well. Everything's fine, my paintings are starting to attract attention in a gallery in SoHo, in Manhattan. I've sold four. But besides that, I've fallen in love, and you know that love makes us selfish. Anyway, it won't be long before I come to see you. Love from, Your daughter."

I got out of the car and crossed the garden stealthily, looking in all directions. No-one. There was a full moon. On the outside envelope I'd written "Ramiro Núñez". On the inside one, nothing. I tiptoed up the steps, and dropped the double message into a green painted letter box that stuck out from the wall next to the Lady of Perpetual Help. Crickets chirped.

"Now I can forget about that for a while," I thought with relief, pulling back on to the main road. When I got home I was exhausted.

XI

Tip of the Iceberg

The voices of the past climb up one's back like a sudden gust of wind. We are like mountains whose facing slopes, more fertile but more vulnerable, are defended by fortifications and covered in gardens, homes, paths and warehouses; there we learn what's known, we fear what's not known, and life is ruled by interlinking laws; no-one looks at the other slope, it's harder to reach from the valley (according to the maps), the sun almost never shines there, and the vegetation is sparse. We end up forgetting that the other slope exists. Even so, it gets attacked by the phantom armies of the past, barely perceptibly, like a tickling sensation. They've never made it round to the front, they can't do me any harm – that's what we say when we experience these vague symptoms – they don't merit our attention, they'll go away just as they came, of their own accord. Nonetheless we protect our bellies and our chests with our arms, close our eyes and prick up our ears, holding our breath. They tend to take advantage of those distracted moments that precede or invite sleep, when we've already cleared our mental attics: I don't want to think about that, or about that either, it's like pushing buttons and pulling out plugs so all the machines stop humming. Then you feel the subtle rattling up the spine, it's nothing. But there it stays. What are those voices saying? To pose the question is to yield to the danger. Who's speaking? Where from? The question seems to come from a mouth so close that the words it utters are drowned out by faltering breathing. But also from far away, and this blend of distance and proximity slips like a drug into the blood. Echoes that disturb and excite, we try in vain to dispel them, tell me more, I can't quite hear you, who are you, come closer.

"It's me, Rosario Tena, are you there? . . . OK. You're not there, or you don't want to answer, same thing. Remember me? The teacher with the granny glasses . . . Look, I don't want to sound bitter. In a couple of days I'm leaving for Santander, I'll be staying there for the summer or maybe forever. Before that I need to see you, it's outrageous that we haven't seen each other. Whatever it takes, please call me, it's the fourth time I've tried to reach you. Kisses. *Ciao*."

That's the message I found waiting on my machine that night when I got back from the Indian settlement. I listened to it when I was already in bed, with my eyes closed. I hit the button and turned my back on it. It had been recorded not long before, perhaps while I'd been talking to Dad about Rosario in fact, but the urgency and haste of her message, the complaint and even the slight sarcasm – perfectly understandable! – from someone who was suffering and who missed me, who had surely not stopped caring about me, were cruelly left out in the cold, defused, I'll think about it tomorrow.

But, even so, the past and its armies climbed up the one phrase that had unsettled me, "whatever it takes". When Rosario had said it, she'd imitated Mum's voice, that tone so much her own, a combination of cynicism, humour and impatience with which she confronted incompetence, cowardice or a slowness to respond, "Please, whatever it takes!" She never made indecisions, nor did she delay in carrying out a task she'd agreed to do, and if she was deceived, she looked the person in the eye. She knew how to get out of quagmires alone, and she also made her mistakes alone. My mother had started down the consoling path that led into the dense woods of metaphor, it would be futile to phone her, she'd hidden down there.

"I'll go down to the woods tonight," I murmured, already half-asleep, "I want to see you, nothing else matters. Whatever it takes, I have to find you in the woods."

I fell asleep straight away, but our encounter must have taken place close to morning. People who write essays on the dream-world say that these lengths of time cannot be measured no matter how tenaciously we stick a ruler into the deep and murky waters ("Oh, Innana, don't go investigating the secrets of the nether-world!"), although they suspect – yes, indeed – that down there everything can happen in just a few upper-world seconds, a plot with preamble, climax and dénouement, as well as extraneous details that shed no light, as if hidden within us we had a novelist whose face we never see, but who, as soon as we close our eyes, hits the ground running. And always leaves us thirsting for another chapter.

I was going to see Mum. Someone must have given me her address, I don't know who, it was a shadowy business, I only know that I arrived at night, frightened, walking on slippery terrain, and under a street light I looked at a piece of paper resembling the map my father had drawn for me with directions to the Indian settlement, but the words had been smudged by the rain. Mum was living incognito, in a hideout on the wrong side of the tracks, ashamed that she hadn't died and fearful of the trouble she'd cause if she was discovered. She didn't have any papers, she'd grown older and was sharing her life with a guy who looked like Félix, who mistreated her and forced her to work as a tightrope walker in a circus. "Just think, if anything happened," she told me, "we don't even have health insurance." The place was a sort of house on stilts over a dirty river, accessed by some rudimentary planks that served as a bridge. She turned pale when she saw me and beseeched me with clasped hands not to tell anyone she was still alive, "Whatever it takes please, I beg you," but there was no laughter or cynicism in her voice, only terror. Her shoulders shook and she spoke in a very low voice, looking over at Félix, who was lying face down on the floor, possibly drunk. I knew everything would be all right if she and I embraced, but I was incapable of approaching her or of saying an affectionate word even though I wanted to very much.

I woke up and felt for my diary to write down the dream, but as I touched it inside my bag that was lying on the carpet (reaching my diary was turning out to be as difficult as kissing Mum), I realised there was someone in the house and that their noise was what had awakened me. Someone stopped outside the bedroom door.

"Tomás!" I exclaimed. "Thank goodness you've come back!"

But I realised straight away that it wasn't Tomás. He never knocked.

"Come in! . . . Oh, it's you, Remedios, good morning. What are you doing here?"

"This is my day to be here. It's Tuesday."

She was stout and spoke with a Galician accent, the doorman's sister-in-law. She'd been coming in to clean our flat twice a week for two-and-a-half years now, and she was determined to teach me how to cook, a frankly commendable obstinacy if you took my disinterest into account.

"Tuesday?" I asked, glancing sidelong at my diary, which I'd managed to rescue from the conjurer's bag, along with a pen.

"Yes, Señorita. All day. What's the matter? Aren't you going to work today? It's after 10.00. You're not ill, are you?"

(The dream! It was urgent. I had to decode the dream. I felt as if I was reflected in a mirror, but from the wrong side.)

"A little. That must be why I thought yesterday was Sunday, because I didn't go to work, I wasn't feeling well . . . Was that yesterday? Yes, of course, yesterday."

Along with scenes from the recent past, various dilemmas

began to present themselves. I should phone the Archive. And there was that message from Rosario, poor Rosario, she'd probably slept badly. What did I have against her anyway?

"Well, a friend of yours was buzzing here yesterday afternoon and no-one answered. Weren't you home?"

"I must've been asleep. What friend?"

"I don't know. She left this envelope with my sister-in-law. She says the woman was very nice. With grey hair, she said."

I took it. It was quite a bulky manilla envelope. The return address was Magda's, my colleague at the Archive. What a busybody, if she hadn't come over, she'd have burst from curiosity.

"Oh, right, it's from work. I'll open it later," I said grumpily.

"OK, I've brought some grapefruit. Do you want me to make you some juice?"

"Yes, please. Thanks."

"I don't know how you can want something so sour, when there's a piece of *tarta de Santiago* . . ."

She left and I put Magda's envelope on the floor. I didn't want to be distracted by subplots until I'd written down the dream, it was too strange to be allowed to escape. But it had already been contaminated a little by the untimely light of that Tuesday, and the scene, somewhat frayed around the edges, began to grow weeds and confusing connections. In any case the gigolo who looked like Félix was still lying face down on the floor, unmoving. Someone, maybe me, was shining a torch on him saying: "Nobody touch anything!" a phrase that hadn't appeared in the dream. I'd seen too many films, I thought. My mother's hideout (my mother who, of course, was growing ever more blurred) was exactly like that of Richard Widmark in the Sam Fuller movie *Pickup on South Street*. I wrote all this down in the section of my diary entitled 'EXCRESCENCES'. One day I must amplify these summaries and write them out properly, there are some very odd things among them. It took only the thought to realise I'd never do it, so I discarded the idea. Then I went into the bathroom.

Once under the shower, which always inspires me, I kept thinking about the eternal circular connection between cinema, dreams, behaviour and the interpretation of reality. On saying "Rosario Tena", for example, I almost never thought about the lecturer who, during the last year of my degree, came to substitute for the Art History professor, that girl, not much older than me, not shy, not pedantic, thin, with granny glasses. She expressed herself with passion and clarity in front of the slides of paintings, following the lines of a landscape or a face with long fingers, as if she was telling stories to a child. If those attributes had disappeared – I said to myself as the water ran over my naked body, which I could see reflected in the wall mirror – the blame lay with Joseph Mankiewicz. Ever since, a few years later (when I was already living in the blue-papered garret), my mother had admitted her to the upper part of the maisonette where she'd installed her new studio, Rosario had taken on the features and gestures of Anne Baxter, that supposedly ingenuous but actually perfidious admirer who ends up supplanting Bette Davis in one of the movies I've seen most often: *All About Eve*. And as I looked at myself in the mirror, I put on a questioning face, good grief, realising this with such clarity at that precise moment carried a charge like dynamite: who creates coincidences like these? But we don't know anything about anything, everything's waiting to be discovered, every once in a while the tip of an iceberg peeks out, and we strut around as if it existed thanks to us. Yes, it was because of *All About Eve*, imagine that. Everything I didn't know about the friendship between Mum and Rosario I had subconsciously invented along the lines of a screenplay enacted by two women's faces in black and white. And remembering the lecturer with the granny glasses, whose hurt voice had been recorded so recently on the answering machine, I was alarmed by my permanent and vicious fixation on the unreal.

In the mirror, splattered with droplets, Mum's face, topping my nude body, lit up with a teasing look that dissolved my anxiety. She shook her wet hair.

"So, I'm Bette Davis, then, am I? Have a look, do you see any bulging eyes?"

I approached the mirror, laughing too. We were identical.

"Well no, frankly. You're gorgeous and quite rejuvenated. What a relief that the Félix thing was a dream! You don't live with him, do you?"

"I don't know who Félix is. When you start raving, you can't be left on your own. Imagine thinking of poor Rosario as a criminal! Let's see if you can't pay her a bit of attention, she's having a really hard time. And if you care to remember, the person who stuck her in my house was you. You said she was marvellous. You get these ideas in your head . . ."

I went up to the mirror and planted my lips over my reflection. It was the reconciliation that had been left hanging in the dream.

"What a pleasure to have you telling me off and being so lively, Mum! Come back again tonight, OK? But without Félix this time. I have to leave you now. Domestic matters, you know."

Remedios, the housekeeper, had been outside the door trying to get my attention for a while. I turned off the water, waved goodbye to my reflection, put on my robe and went out. I was ready to be nice to everyone.

"What's up Remedios? Did you say something?"

She was standing in the middle of the bedroom, wearing an expression of profound shock.

"Yes, I did. What's happened in the kitchen?"

"In the kitchen? I don't know. Has something broken?"

"Broken no. But the blender's gone, the food processor, all the knives and . . . well, why bother listing them, all the utensils and gadgets."

"Oh right! I thought it was something else."

"Something else? Well, the whole kitchen is something else entirely, nobody would recognise it, Señorita, forgive me for saying so. If you want to leave it as it is, fine, I won't interfere, but where are you going to cook? And I'm not talking about a proper Galician stew like God intended, but even a simple omelette."

As I accompanied her to the area of contention, I tried to explain that it was just a temporary change, and to make my assertion more believable I applied myself without delay to clearing the table and taking books and utensils back to their original locations, which (as always happens) was never quite the same; and so, by depositing them in another place, they were imbued with loss.

Remedios, who followed me while talking incessantly, took advantage of my unusually compliant mood, and let fly a list of advice, messages and small grievances that had been building up for several weeks.

So, from that moment until I left the house a little over an hour later, without really knowing where I was going, the fragments of all those pending matters fought for my attention, suggestions and reflexes from each cancelling out the next.

It was horribly hot again.

I arrived at the terrace bar of the Bellas Artes around midday with a splitting headache, ordered an iced coffee and opened Magda's manilla envelope.

The first thing I took out was a handwritten note from her:

"I enclose," it said, "these photocopies sent by my friend Emma, the professor at the University of Barcelona I told you about, which I hope will keep you from getting bored while you recover. I imagine you'll be interested to discover Vidal y Villalba wasn't Italian, as he wanted people to believe, but the son of humble artisans from Barcelona. There are lots of other details, all quite juicy, about the deeds of your beloved rascal. The only problem is that the article's in Catalan, and I forget if this is one of your languages. In any case, if you happen to need a Catalan dictionary, call me, because I've got one and it would be no problem at all to bring it over to you. Hope you're feeling better. Hugs, Magda."

There was also a handwritten index card clipped to the photocopies. The writing was different, flatter. It said:

> From the book *Vuit segles de cultura catalana a Europa*, ed. Biblioteca Selecta, Barcelona, 1958, pp. 159–166. Sorry it's taken me so long to send it, but I've been swamped with work. I hope it's of use to your friend. Fond regards, Emma.

"Excuse me," said the waiter, who'd just come over with my iced coffee. "If you don't move your papers, they're going to get dirty. It's a small table."

"Yes, and wobbly," I said, as I tried to make a bit of space.

"Well, that can be fixed."

I got in a bit of a muddle with my bag and the papers, some of which fell on the ground. I bent down to pick them up and my hands brushed those of the waiter, who had knelt down to prop up the table with the folded cover of a book of matches.

I came back up to the surface, stifled and gasping.

"It never rains but it pours . . ." I grumbled.

"Relax, love, don't get rattled." The young man smiled, our brief encounter under the table seeming to have given him a pretext to drop the usual waiter-customer formalities. "That'll be 400 pesetas, if you don't mind paying me now. But relax, there's no hurry."

I'd just read the title of the article and didn't know what to focus on.

"I am relaxed," I said, taking out my purse. "The thing is, I'm surrounded by the tips of icebergs."

The waiter laughed.

"That wouldn't be such a bad thing, given the temperature out here. Though I assume you're speaking metaphorically."

"Yes, sweetheart, I am." I smiled. "You like metaphors?"

"Well, I practise them in my spare time. They help keep things in perspective. Our trade union's plagued with poets, you'll discover that as soon as you start looking," he said as he picked up the tray.

"Yeah. I'd noticed."

I gave him a decent tip. Someone called him from another table and I returned avidly to my task. The photocopied article was entitled, "*Lluís Vidal, català extra-vagant*", and offered a very stimulating opening:

'Extra-vagant, en el sentit etimològic del terme, I extravagant de tarannà, l'aventurer Lluís Vidal és l'exageració d'un tipus molt català . . .'

I didn't know the word *tarannà*. I drank my iced coffee, and after a brief pause put the papers in my conjurer's bag and stood up decisively.

"Finally, the course of this odd morning is taking shape," I thought as I crossed at the lights to the odd-numbered side of Alcalá, where it turned into Gran Vía. The top half of Gran Vía was the best, I wasn't in a hurry, what a pleasure to have left the car at home, 36 degrees centigrade read the thermometer on top of the Grassy Jeweller's building. Well, that's summer. I walked happily along the pavement in the shade, looking at the coats of arms and balconies on the buildings every now and then. How refined, how modern this avenue must have been when Alfonso XIII inaugurated it at the beginning of the century! And how decadent it was now, so abandoned, as invaded by cash machines as it was by beggars, tinned grandeur and raw misery. But those reflections, which helped to calm the rhythm of my steps, didn't divert me from my objective. My destination was the Espasa Calpe bookshop. I needed a Catalan dictionary in a hurry. The tips of all the other icebergs disappeared.

XII

The Living Statue

Sometimes the city seems to turn physically upsetting, and arriving at a certain street corner you're assaulted by a mysterious pain, like a punch in the stomach.

When I came out of the Espasa Calpe with my new Catalan dictionary in a little transparent bag, my whole being was a balloon escaped from the hands of a child. All I knew was that I didn't feel like going home and that I was in flight, drifting away from any plan, even that of finding a place to sit down and eat and perhaps begin to make the translation that had recently seemed so urgent. How well I know that burning rush to lay the first brick at the base of a structure often left unbuilt. In other words, nothing to get alarmed about. I carried my small red brick enclosed in its wrapper, and I felt good, the city wasn't hurting or oppressing me. I walked along, lost among the other people, at a lazy pace, concentrating obsessively on the word *tarannà*, as though it was a catchy chorus stuck in my head, displacing and nullifying any other thought. Before buying the dictionary, I had opened it to the Ts, and discovered that *tarannà* meant "character", "nature". So Vidal y Villalba was extravagant by *tarannà*; I liked having learned a new word that had invaded my cerebral machinations, annihilating the tiniest malignant seed of worry; *tarannà*, it amused me and kept me company like a new friend encountered by chance. Regarding my own *tarannà* I don't know much, but it doesn't matter, we're going along up Gran Vía, wait, red light, *tarannà*, *tarannà*, *tarannà*. Sometimes it sounded a bit like *tarambana*, that scatterbrained Don Luis's *tarannà*, other times like nothing, just a drum roll, with me marching to its beat, swinging the little bag containing the book from whose pages came this friendly word that had begun my pleasant stroll. And on I went until I reached the corner by the Santo Domingo metro.

At that side street came the blow that still hurts when I remember it from a distance of two-and-a-half years, however much I try to think of other things, a scar that ached again. "Looks like we're in for a change in the weather," they usually say in such circumstances. They don't mean meteorology when they use that phrase, but other kinds of pressure systems. We refer to "time passed since the accident" and what we relive, touching the scar, is the accident itself, and the changes occasioned since the day it happened.

I saw him in the distance before I crossed the road, standing on a little bench, immobile, dressed as a devil. People were stopping to look at him, two years ago street artists weren't, like now, an integral part of the urban landscape, they were isolated and startling exceptions. They attracted attention, just as they still seek to but with less success today. His face was covered with black shoe polish and he wore a snug helmet with horns, it was also black, as were his hands, his feet and a short cape. But his tight leotard was red. He brandished a trident.

I approached him with a mixture of curiosity and apprehension and stopped a few steps away. The first thought I had was that he must be terribly hot in his disguise, with those flannel gloves, and then the added torment of the make-up and the effort of not moving a single muscle. He was in the shade, of course, but still. I looked to see if he had a tail, and he did, a bushy one, of imitation fox fur. How odd! And wings too. That was the prettiest part, a pair of membranous wings stuck to the cape, like those of an enormous insect, but uneven. The right one was slightly broken and drooping. It seemed as though it had been devised that way on purpose, perhaps a homage to Lucifer's misfortune at being cast out of Paradise. The mime must have been uncomfortable, leaning back, somewhat off balance.

At last I looked at his face, and froze into a statue myself. Despite the fact that it was half-covered by the hand that wasn't holding the trident, and considering that the black make-up could be deceptive, he looked so much like Roque that it was Roque. Was I really seeing him or was it a hallucination? "He invents other things so he can keep pretending to be someone else," Félix had told me a few days earlier. "His imagination runs wild." I knew that all too well; it was what I'd liked about him from the day I first met him, we were united by a refusal to be controlled by anyone, much less by each other, we laughed at couples who tried to share everything at the expense of their own freedom, who spied on or lectured each other. Later – I must confess – I was guilty of exactly that when I began to suffer atrocious attacks of jealousy, when I got my wing broken and was expelled from Paradise, these things happen, they happened, no-one's to blame, better not to delve into them.

I didn't dare stare at him. I'd seen only the slightest static brilliance in his blank eyes, noted his grin and his arm at a right angle half-covering his sharp nose. Was it him? I wasn't entirely sure, and that uncertainty accentuated the "corner pain", which is what I've come to call it since that July morning: a piece of street that pierces you.

And naturally, I didn't dare ask him anything, statue that he was. It wasn't just the embarrassment of doing so in front of the people who'd stopped, like me, to look at him, nor the distance between our bodies created by his immobility and that empty gaze, but also – and this was worse – the way time had put the screws on, that's what hurt, the years since our last fight, the one that separated us for good, the resentment at that old wound. I was ashamed to recall the vulgar and inexcusable scene provoked by me and doomed to end in disaster, a futile attempt to stir the embers of a dying fire, a wild attack of *amour-propre* and loneliness, a terrible combination, as I knew even before I showed up at his house; but hearing him say so made me see red, "Unbecoming of you, honey." He smiled, and I broke a vase like in the movies.

I'd never been in that room before, he used to come to the blue-papered garret, sometimes he'd move in for a while, I boasted of my horror at interfering in anybody's life, and never wanted to set foot in his flat, which he shared with a younger brother, who'd come out rather shocked at the noise of pottery smashing on the floor. But Roque didn't even look at the shards, just moved one or two disdainfully with his foot, "Unbecoming of you, honey," and smiled.

Timidly, I searched out his smile, barely sketched behind that black flannel glove, and it was quite similar, or maybe not, whenever I try to make judgements of this kind the Mona Lisa always gets in the way; it was the painting Rosario Tena examined most carefully when she was the girl with the granny glasses I liked so much; there were traces of that immortal smile in the turn of Roque's mocking mouth, but he'd get the devil in him when he heard me say so – maybe the devil had finally possessed him and had stuck him on a corner of Gran Vía – he couldn't stand the Mona Lisa, he thought it was wonderful that Marcel Duchamp had painted a moustache on her, "That lecturer of yours must be a bit affected, isn't she, going on about the Mona Lisa." "Yeah, and you don't go on about Duchamp." "Touché," he'd admit. And we'd laugh.

"Looks real," said a woman in black standing beside me.

"You're silly, Mum, what do you mean real!" said the young girl with her.

"You don't think so? They'll try anything. He's not sweating."

"But he just blinked. He's real, I tell you."

"Don't be so sure," I interrupted. "Some dolls blink too."

And I knew I'd spoken so that Roque, if it were Roque, would hear my voice. "It's the most unusual thing about you," he told me one day, "I'd recognise it anywhere, no matter how many years had passed." But he didn't move a muscle. Not even at the sound of the coin the girl dropped into the saucer before being dragged away by her mother.

"You shouldn't have given him anything," she was saying.

"Why not? He's an artist."

"Oh yes, brave artist. As long as he doesn't have to work for a living like God intended . . ."

Other passers-by put money in the little plate, and he remained impassive, looking away at nothing, keeping the raised arm from trembling. I'd spent too long stuck there, waiting for a miracle that was obviously not going to occur, but I didn't leave. I was afraid I was infected by his frozen state and the fear began to stiffen my limbs, I was incapable of shouting for help, although I was sure someone would notice. My entire being seemed to be losing its strength, I needed to hear the ambulance siren, why weren't they helping me, I was bleeding in the middle of the road. But everything stayed the same, the devil didn't move and I didn't move, surrounded by distracted, indifferent people, who scattered banal observations as if they were wandering among stone statues in a cemetery.

Maybe it wasn't Roque. I lowered my eyes and fancied that his ankles looked thicker, or perhaps they were swollen from standing for so long. I no longer dared to look at his face. But what if it was him? Then it would be horrible. If it's him and he doesn't know me and doesn't look at me – I thought – I'll also have dreamt I had a mother, that I learned Russian, that I studied Art History and wrote inter-rock songs, that I like grapefruit juice, that I've spent many nights crying when no-one can see me. It'll be as if a sponge soaked in vinegar erased from the blackboard of my past every trace of chalk, any illusion of growth, all the connections of one episode with another, hope will turn to smoke, disappointment to lies. And daring – that willingness to play at whatever comes up, to keep betting on the unknown, all the love of risk Roque encouraged in me – reduced to a mistaken code. And my body and his a lie, my word and his. And death a lie as well.

We'd been left alone facing one another. It was time to say goodbye. My heart beat as hard as the first time I'd seen him, leaning against the bar in the *Fuego Fatuo*, alone, wearing a pale scarf, and I'd known straight away that he was mine, part of my life. He hadn't looked at me that night either, nor did he do so for several weeks. It took him many more to confess he'd more than seen me, that he'd awaited my arrival anxiously and observed me surreptitiously as I did him. Or maybe that too was a lie.

I risked raising my eyes and looked for the ears I'd kissed so often, small, brazen, unmistakable, but they were tucked up under the devil's cap.

I edged over to the wall and leaned against it, not far from his body, feeling faint. My head came up to his elbow because of the bench. His clothes didn't smell of anything. I looked at his profile.

"Roque," I managed to get out, not very loud or very quiet. "Goodbye, good luck. And I'm sorry I broke the vase that day."

He didn't move. So I took my diary out of my bag, tore out a page and wrote down my telephone number. Then, without looking at him, I bent down to put the paper, along with a 500-peseta coin, in the little plate. I felt like kneeling and kissing his feet like a Christ, but they didn't look like his feet, they were disfigured by the pointed shoes with flames drawn on in fluorescent orange. That was rather tacky. Maybe it wasn't Roque. And anyway, who cared?

I walked away without looking back. "The secret of happiness lies in not insisting," I was saying on my way down Gran Vía; I think it's a quote from Gregorio Martínez Sierra, an author I'm told my grandfather liked, my mother had discovered that Don Gregorio's wife, María, had written all of his works, but she didn't want to tell Grandfather because he might be annoyed. Tip of another iceberg, my visit to Grandfather was still pending, I could walk in saying: "The secret of happiness lies in not insisting," and it would be Mum who looked at him, because I haven't read Martínez Sierra, I wonder what would happen if I did that, it was a good idea, but better not to think about my grandfather right now, nor about Ramiro either, too many things. "Happiness, secret, happiness," I repeated to myself as I increased my pace, trying not to zigzag and to control the rhythm of my breathing. I realised that the word *happiness* was a dead weight, so I wrapped it up in an old newspaper and chucked it into the first bin I passed, it smelled bad and was bloodstained. *Secret*, on the other hand, I decided I would keep. "It'll be the last thing I throw away," I promised myself in a whisper, "it'll come to the grave with me, a matter of character, *tarannà*."

I started to feel better. The city was recovering little by little and my footsteps sounded firmer, as I got farther away from the corner where I'd had that harrowing bite to the neck. Past and future secrets spun harmonious webs round the word *tarannà*, and my stroll regained its arbitrariness, its lack of design, *tarannà*, *tarannà*, I let myself wander, irrigating a parched field with the present.

Before I knew it I was sitting on a bench in the Plaza de España, looking at the statues of Don Quixote and Sancho Panza. I didn't like the way that the knight was so far in front and looked so battle-hardened, lance at the ready, leaving the other poor fellow behind. I always imagine them riding side by side so they could hear each other, because if not, fine company they'd be, and the important thing is what they say, the words that live on; what use was it for Japanese tourists to take photos of these statues that didn't commemorate anything? Sancho shrugged his shoulders.

> *But let them say what they will; naked I was born, and naked I am: I can neither lose nor win; and, so my name be but in print, and go about the world from hand to hand, I care not a fig, let people say of me whatever they list.*

I always feel so sorry for statues. So immobile.

On the other hand, my body was loosening up and memories were buzzing around in a throng, as if they all wanted to come out at the same time through too narrow an opening. They were on the move and moving me from within, I felt their vibrations. And threading together those buried memories was like coming back to life. The blackboard of the past began to fill up with chalk marks again.

After the nights that I dreamt of him I wouldn't get out of bed until very late, reluctant to leave the place where the encounter had occurred. It happened sporadically, between the ages of 13 and 18, I think. A dream that continued even after I'd started taking the pill, and which I'd forget from one time to the next until he reappeared. I used to record the date of each dream when I woke up, because at that age I wrote almost everything down. The dates were ever more spread out, but somehow linked to each other. "He was here again," I'd write, "He still exists," or "It's been half a year since he last appeared." And then a character from the Russian alphabet surrounded by little lines like the rays of the sun, because I knew Russian; it would be a different letter each time, but I loved drawing them and colouring them in, it seemed that learning Russian was especially useful for my secrets, especially the one incubated through shadowy tunnels leading out to the light where my nameless friend awaited me. I'd invent a new name for him each time.

One of the few aspects of my education that my father insisted on was my learning Russian from an early age, and for years I was taught by a friend of his who'd recently come back from Moscow, where she'd been exiled with other children since the Civil War. Her name was Mila and she lived in Antón Martín in a miserable flat, not very far, as a matter of fact, from the blue-papered garret where I lived later until I met Tomás. She was patient, melancholic, friendly and of course a very good teacher. But I could barely make myself climb five steep flights of stairs three times a week to that stuffy room that overlooked a dark courtyard and was full of portraits and paper flowers. And Russian was difficult, let's be honest. During those tedious mornings I came to understand for the first time what it meant to inherit something. My father transferred to me his unsatisfied desire to learn a language that was mythic for him, and I inherited, whether I wanted to or not, homage paid to a war not my own, a penance I eventually accepted. But later, that penance (the only one my father inflicted on me) turned itself into a blessing from heaven, because an Art History graduate had slim chances of earning a living and as a musician I was never more than an amateur. On the other hand, good translators from Russian are few and far between, and well paid. Thanks to that I was able to leave home.

But, long before I took that step, being able to draw Russian letters surrounded by sunbeams to symbolise the nocturnal protagonist of my adolescent dreams seemed sufficient reward. The strange thing is that after so many years and so many interludes which should have clouded that hazy leitmotif, it would still resurface every once in a while, a ghostly presence and yet often with the intensity of lived experience, a sensation similar to what (it is said) a blind person feels when trying to remember colours. I don't recall if the physical appearance of that man was the same from one dream to the next, I think what led me to recognise him was what I felt before I saw him, as his protective waves started to reach me, the sense that he was somewhere nearby. I was aware that he didn't dress like everyone else, and I wasn't sure the others in my dream could see him. The plot of those dreams was quite straightforward. Often we'd meet in enclosed places where there were lots of other people, everybody laughing, dancing or looking for someone, but a little lost. I'd see real friends of mine and I would talk to them more than to him. There were usually caves with passageways and the storyline didn't vary much. At other times we'd come to the surface and I'd know we were in Paris, it would be very cold, there were street lamps, I'd never been to Paris, but I recognised the city in those streets and those intense smoke-filled scenes. I'd be scared if I couldn't feel him nearby, even though I was surrounded by friends, even if I were in the arms of one of them. When I saw him at the back of a room or simply noticed he'd come in, that he was there, my fear would vanish, and my eyes would tell him so. And if we went outside, he'd leave with us. I never remembered us having a conversation, only the promise not to let each other down, to meet again one day. They weren't erotic dreams. He never kissed me.

"What's the matter?" Mum sometimes asked, if she came into my room and found me with my head under the sheets.

"Nothing, leave me alone."

"Are you ill or is something wrong?"

"Please, leave me alone."

"I was just going to remind you that today . . ."

"Don't remind me of anything! Close the blinds, please."

Then, during the day, I'd imagine phoning him, almost always at hotels where I couldn't ask for him as I didn't know his name, so I'd hang up as soon as a receptionist, who was usually Mischa

Auer, said "*Allô?*" Or, if I stopped in front of a shop window, I'd close my eyes tightly, certain that on opening them I'd see him reflected behind me. But he never came.

Meanwhile, time passed, I found out quite early what a girl had to do not to get pregnant, I started studying for my degree and proceeded with life's ups and downs, I got pleasure from pleasing (a tendency that has been gradually refined), I abided by the customary code of how to benefit from youth. I knew that almost all people of my age – rhizomorphs or not – had similar problems but preferred to talk about other ones, to disguise ourselves as something we hadn't yet or might never become, and that in that masked ball the only way to survive was by drinking and by showing nerve and mistrust in eternal, Hollywood-style love. I was very successful with men, I knew it. But until that night in the *Fuego Fatuo*, where I went frequently with rhizomorphs of both sexes, when I saw that thin guy with the pale scarf leaning on the bar, it had never occurred to me to link the recurring stranger of my dreams, symbolised on paper by differing Russian characters, with any flesh-and-blood being.

I didn't meet him immediately, nor did I ask anyone his name. I wanted him to coincide for as long as possible with the subterranean apparition who, incidentally, had been denying me his favours for several years. And when, at last, Roque (the first person to tear off the skin of my past and pull out the flesh of an impenitent present) began to look at me and allow me to look at him, I relished the certainty that it was him, the one from my dreams, and years later what glitters and remains from my relationship with Roque is mostly that first stage of silent complicity, the preparations for the voyage. Because later, when the inevitable happened, that haven where I deposited my uncertainties and dreams began to turn – if I have to be truthful – into the unbearable and blind trembling of my body enslaved to the whims of his.

It must have been 5.30 p.m. by the time I stood up from the

bench in the Plaza de España. For a moment I was tempted to go to the Alphaville and see a film to change my mood, but an interior malaise persisted that I knew wouldn't be placated by that, it seemed to demand some other form of distraction, and I found it in the Catalan dictionary. I took it out of its bag right there, in front of the statues of Don Quixote and Sancho, and began to learn about some of Don Luis's wanderings through Martinique, and the name of one of his lovers, Carlota Picolet, who might easily have been the woman in the portrait in the little box he had with him when they took him prisoner, a name out of a novel; and all his entanglements until his death in a prison on the Rock of Gibraltar, delirious by then. It was all rather condensed, because the article was only six pages long, but it was very useful. It was like a canvas on which to embroider the rest of my scattered jottings. I stood up, intending to go and thank Magda and tell her about the developments this information had brought to my research. It would be a way to get back to work and return to harbour, "because you and I, Don Alonso," I said looking at the statue of Don Quixote, "once we mount Clavileño's horse, no-one can get us off, and Don Luis was the same."

I went into a snack bar on Gran Vía to have a hot dog and a glass of beer and suddenly I was very cross about having given Roque my phone number; I'm incorrigible, how do such idiocies occur to me, as if my life weren't already complicated enough. And besides, Roque didn't deserve to be given any chances, end of story, enough idealising. So I went back again towards the corner where I'd seen the devil, with the intention of settling that issue and eradicating its potential harm. If the piece of paper was still in the saucer, that would mean it wasn't Roque, because he would have bent down to pick it up as soon as he saw me disappear. And if the piece of paper had disappeared, I planned to ask him for it back, even if it meant making a scene.

The only thing that was clear to me was that because of the piece of paper my blood was boiling again and I was back in the dangerous labyrinths of obsession, so I went up the hill slowly, uncertain, wanting both to wash my hands of the matter and keep delving into its mysteries. I stopped here and there. Three hours had gone by, and who was to say – my sensible self admonished me – that the devil would still be on the same corner?

But he was still there. And so was the piece of paper, which I dug out from among the coins with tense, rude gestures, huffing with rage. Then I stood up and couldn't help but look at the living statue. This time he was smiling a bit more. It was Roque, no doubt about it.

"You're a swine!" I hissed. "And anyway, I don't know when you've ever protected or consoled me at all. You're not the one from my dream!"

Then I ran off and hailed a taxi.

XIII

Night and Day

"It's all so absurd!" I said to Magda.

She regarded me with a look of incomprehension.

When I appeared, she was already tidying up her desk, and I noted a perceptible alteration to the precise, muted actions from which surfaced, no matter what she was doing, her own *tarannà*. She's 50 years old, and has been, uncomplaining, in this job for more than 20, and if she felt like it she could make my life impossible because, no matter which way you look at it, she's my boss. But in fact I'm the one who takes her down a peg or two when she gets on my nerves. And, what's more, I have no qualms about brazenly exploiting the blend of admiration and maternal instinct that makes her forgive all my faults.

That afternoon, when our eyes met, I felt like a despicable worm. Perhaps seven hours had gone by (calculating it accentuated my misconduct) since Remedios had handed me the manilla envelope that set me off on my recent urban wanderings, and I thought bitterly of my attack of ingratitude and disdain at finding out that Magda had called on me. She, however, showed no sign of paying me back in kind. Looking at her, I was aware of that part of myself which accuses and attacks when exposed. It was all absurd, the vacillations of my behaviour as much as my attempts to justify or understand them. As I got into the taxi and gave the address of the Archive between laboured breaths, I'd wondered at my vehement decision. With Tomás away, where to direct my steps? I couldn't imagine at that moment, miraculously liberated from the clutches of the devil, any place more secure against external threats and my own neurosis than that office; I needed to see the ordered papers and the unchanging expression of their keeper in order to quieten my soul and ensure that each of those scenes swirling around inside me went back into its box, if only for a while. I could see an X-ray of my insides like this, a living space plagued by disarray, disordered and bursting cupboards spilling their contents on the floor in disastrous confusion.

Thank goodness I'd arrived in time. It was 6 p.m. and she's always the last to leave. The taxi driver had good luck with the traffic lights.

"What's absurd?" asked Magda, who obviously hadn't quite registered my appearance. "Has something happened to you? Sit down, you don't look well."

Her face lit up with a sudden smile. I'd set that morning's manilla envelope down on the table along with the Catalan dictionary, and that gave her an excuse to change the conversation's direction, grabbing hold of the end of a familiar thread.

"How's Don Luis?" she asked. "Was that article Emma sent any use to you?"

"Oh yes, it's a real find. I came here to thank you, you never let anyone down when they ask you for a favour. It gives lots of clues about his time in South America and London, and then his final madness, which is really bleak, 17 years spent in various prisons without anyone knowing exactly why they were holding him, can you imagine, and in the end he lost his mind completely, said he was a prince, that he was the son of the Queen of Heaven, his mania for grandeur had taken over. He died in 1803 on Gibraltar completely detached from all logic. It's a very sad story."

Magda looked at me uneasily, as if waiting.

"Well, I'm pleased you've found it useful. Let's see if you don't decide at last to start writing."

"I don't know," I said, "I doubt it."

"Why?"

"I don't know what's wrong with me, Magda, I'm more confused every day. I know other researchers concentrate on their theme, get to the point and that's it, they can separate it out from the rest. But I can't. For me everything's important."

"From the rest? What do you mean?"

"I don't know, I mean a bit of everything, like when what happens to me at each moment gets mixed up in my head with what happened to me before, and with other people's stories, living, dead, ghosts, scenes from movies, everything folded up together in a mess, so much so that I say to myself: It's not worth separating things out from other things, what's the point? And this research, no matter how exciting I sometimes find it, as you know, other times I can't face it, Don Luis is a tumour grabbing me from within, I have to stop thinking about him, you know? Because he leaps through my intestines and I feel it as if he were tearing at my organs. Anyway, sorry, I'm bothering you, Magda, I'm so selfish, you probably have to go home."

She shook her head. I'd let that last spiel fly while I walked around the room, as if talking to myself, and now I stopped in front of her. She looked overwhelmed, plunged into the kind of disorientation that frightens those used to travelling with a compass at all times. She'd stopped organising the folders on her desk and gestured to me to sit down again. I did so with my head bowed, and there was a silence.

"But . . ." she said, as if trying to put two and two together. "So, you weren't ill?"

"Well, no, you see, that's another thing. I didn't have the flu, and last night when you came over I'd gone out. And I don't really know why, because everything I do comes out backwards, my wires get crossed. And on top of that, I blame others for my own cowardice, for finding myself at dead ends, for the scrapes

I get myself into to avoid responsibilities. Every day that goes by I end up with more things to do. So this afternoon I said to myself I'm going to go over and tell Magda I lied to her and apologise. Because listen, I don't know if I'm catching it off Don Luis, but lately I tell a lot of lies, almost without being aware of it, and sometimes about stupid things, which is the worst. I wonder when I started lying. When I was little I never lied."

Whichever way you looked at it, this was beginning to head down the kind of rough paths that lead to the psychiatrist's couch. I realised with amazement that it was the first time I'd confided in Magda, despite the danger involved, given her tendency to confide in me and her eagerness for me to do the same. And the surprising thing is it didn't annoy me but made me feel relieved, who would have guessed it? I noticed she blushed a little, like someone offered an unexpected gift and unsure whether to accept or refuse what might be a mirage.

Her widowed mother, with whom she'd lived for many years, had died shortly after I'd started working at the Archive, and my later bereavement suggested points of contact between us which she took pleasure in encouraging with questions and condolences which got on my nerves and on which I slammed the door with my sharp replies. She was used to me not telling her anything about my life by now, and to considering me a being from another galaxy, isolated within an impregnable fortress. We broadcast – as she put it – on different frequencies. But in this remark of hers there was no detectable resentment, but rather fascination.

I searched for a way to erase the perplexed look from her face, and resorted to one of our office's linguistic complicities that had made her laugh at other times. And in doing so I was asking her a favour, showing her a sign of trust.

"Hey, I know you don't like it, but, I'm d.f.a.s., it happens when I talk a lot."

She did laugh, and took an ashtray out of the drawer. D.f.a.s.

stood for "dying for a smoke". I lit that cigarette with true delight. Magda's eyes followed the spirals of smoke like the traces of hieroglyphs.

"I don't know what to say to you," she said after a silence. "You know I'm a simple person and with you, unintentionally, I end up putting my foot in it. In any case, in human terms, I've always considered you to be very sure of yourself, one of the most self-confident women I know, someone who knows more than most what she wants and why she behaves as she does."

"Well, now you see . . ." I shrugged.

A wave of melancholy engulfed me, as I recalled how many people had that impression of me. But not my mother. She knew very well that it was false, the plagiarised are always the first to notice those who copy them. But, although I knew she thought it, she never confessed it to me clearly, she never said, "Deep down you don't know what you want!" And her silence irritated me, as perhaps mine did her, come to think of it. I wrote several letters to her before leaving home, and later too, letters I was suddenly anxious to re-read. Would she have destroyed them? She wasn't much of a one for keeping old papers. Rosario might know where she kept her private mementoes, there must be some secret drawer in that new dwelling I hadn't been able to stand for more than four months, as unencumbered with furniture as it was lacking in nooks and crannies and hiding places, aseptic and luminous, with an enormous studio. I needed to see Rosario. Although, come to think of it, I write a lot of letters and never end up sending them. They live within me for a time, I repeat their text to the point where I forget I've not sent them, and keep adding a reply against which I've already immunised myself. Maybe I had some of those letters lost in a drawer somewhere or maybe I'd torn them up.

"It could also be that you're upset, no?" Magda ventured cautiously. "We all have days like that. It happens to me too.

Even though I may seem calm to you, often I go home at night and cry my eyes out. I know nobody's circumstances are the same as anyone else's, but losing your mother is always a terrible blow, they carried us inside their bodies for nine months, whichever way you look at it, and that isn't something you get over at the drop of a hat. They're gone and they leave you maimed, that's the moment when you start to age. Still, I'm glad you came, it's a sign of trust. I have very few friends. You must have so many."

"Don't be so sure."

She drank a glass of mineral water, as if she'd exerted herself excessively. Perhaps she feared that I'd react inconsiderately, as I had at other times when she'd tried to compare her orphanhood to mine. But it didn't happen. That afternoon her voice was like balm to me, and I wanted her to ask me more questions. I kept thinking about those uncensored letters I might have sent to Mum during my stormy adolescence, letters she never replied to with the unconditional love I sought. But it wasn't her fault. There are no faults, only causes.

"Sometimes I think," I reflected out loud, "that one lies out of an inability to beg others to accept you as you are. Once you stop admitting your own vulnerability, you disguise yourself as someone else. Then you get a knack for invention and from there on in it's pure deviation, you stagger around with a mask on, getting further away from the path that might lead to self-awareness. That's what happened to Don Luis, you know, I'm realising it more and more clearly, a craving for appreciation or whatever you want to call it."

"Leave Don Luis out of this!" said Magda. "I think you're much more suited to writing poems, you say such strange things I can't follow you, but they're the kind of things that leave you trembling, like poetry that one only half understands. I've been reading St John of the Cross in the evenings, 'and they keep babbling bits of mystery', it's just wonderful. You already know

I'm religious, I've told you that when I was young I almost became a nun."

"I'm religious too in my own way. I mean, I don't go to Mass, but I believe in the world beyond and all that."

"Yes . . ." she said pensively.

A strange silence threatened to drown the conversation. But then Magda channelled it once again. She propped her elbows on the table between us and leaned towards me. I could read an intense curiosity in her round face.

"Forgive me," she said, "I know you don't like anyone meddling in your life, if you don't want to, don't answer me, but . . . do you lie to your husband too?"

"Sometimes. And it's absolutely unforgivable, when I think of it I get enraged, because he's the most reliable, warmest man I've ever met in my entire life, I don't know how he puts up with me, to tell you the truth. When I met him I was a wreck, fit for the rubbish truck, as bad as it could be, and you can't imagine how he straightened me out, but not in a paternalistic way, not in a macho way either, things just went along in the most natural way, bit by bit. With him that's how it is. If you asked me, 'How did he manage it?' I wouldn't know how to answer you, it all comes down to the way he takes me as I am but doesn't let me get away with any old thing, what he thinks can be solved he argues about, stubbornly at times, but he's so patient! And being patient with me is not easy, believe me, because I'm a tough nut to crack. You know what he said to me when we'd only just met? It's incredible."

"What did he say?"

"I didn't know him at all, I'm telling you, never seen him before, it was quite late, I noticed he was next to me in one of those bars in Huertas, and before I realised it, I had unleashed some intolerable tirade in his direction, because when I drink I'm hopeless. But I hadn't been paying proper attention to him – as a man, I mean – he didn't interrupt or abandon me in mid-sentence, like most people I knew, who would disappear on the way from one bar to the next, which is normal, of course, I do it too, if you rise to the bait of every drunk who sticks to you like a limpet and tells you tales of their glories or martyrdoms you'll end up in the madhouse. Well anyway, not to bore you, we ended up at his flat late at night, with me absolutely plastered, it was one of those times when the last thing you feel like doing is going home, because you can't stand yourself. I was starting to think about moving to a new flat, a boyfriend had left me, my whole life was a mess, I was in debt, didn't want to ask my mother for help out of pride, I was floundering . . . and well, I ended up at his place, just as I could have ended up at any other, a Saturday, you know how those Saturday nights end."

"No, I don't. I never go out at night."

"I don't either now, Madrid is so dull. But I'm talking about eight years ago or so, oh God, can it be that long? It's scary how time flies by, eight years! Yes, eight years, because my brother Esteban had just been born."

"But anyway, tell me what you were going to say," Magda said.

She'd taken out her contact lenses, which she had started wearing at my suggestion, and had still not got used to. She put them away in their little case and put on her glasses. I remembered, before continuing, that the story of how I met Tomás ended with one of those phrases that would make you cry if you heard it in a movie, and it dawned on me that I'd heard it from the lips of a flesh-and-blood person "who still exists," I thought, "who still loves me, I've got no proof he's involved with anyone in Jaén." And looking into Magda's blue eyes behind her glasses, so expectant and sympathetic, the statue of the devil crumbled like a hallucination made of sand, an illusion, as was the emphasis on the complicated, the dark and the corrosive that had been common to many of my friends before Tomás. Back then there'd been so much shadowy drama, most of it bad, pure trash. Tomás, who hates shadows, had brought me out into the light, because he emits light. But we take light for granted, we fail to give it the attention it deserves, let it drift off and be swallowed up like waste. I was excited because I'd just made a startling discovery: more than anyone, Tomás resembled the man from my adolescent dreams. I'd been blind. It was him.

"What's the matter?" asked Magda. "Don't you want to tell me what happened then? You're going to leave me halfway through the story?"

I sighed. Yes, of course I wanted to tell her. Most of all, to hear it myself.

"Nothing happened really, I threw up, and he made me coffee and took off my shoes, all the while observing me more than talking, 'lie down, relax,' he said. And he didn't seem as though he wanted to take advantage of me, you know what I mean, you notice that quickly enough no matter how far gone you are. He intrigued me, but I was focused on myself, on getting comfortable so my head would stop spinning and the stabbing pains that wouldn't let me open my eyes would go away. So, I fell asleep on his couch without even finishing the coffee, and at dawn I woke up terrified by a nightmare, I have lots of horrible ones – you know those ones where you're falling and falling and you never stop falling – and I didn't know how to call him because I couldn't remember his name, I didn't even know if he'd told it to me. And I saw him sitting nearby, his back to me, drawing at an angled board, because he's an architect. He's taken that table to his studio now. The light was very soft, greenish, and I got up and put my arms around him, trembling with fear. He seemed to have stayed up all night making changes to a plan. He likes to take advantage of his insomnia to work. 'But, what is it you're afraid of?' he asked me, affectionately, but without groping me or anything like that. And I realised that the thought of leaving there terrified me. 'Of going home,' I said, 'that's what I'm afraid of, and also of daytime, of the light of another day.' 'Really? I find the light comforting,' he said, 'I always want to see the sun rise.' He didn't ask me if I was mistreated at home, or who I lived with. He just said, 'Well, don't go then, if you don't want to. Staying here won't oblige you to do anything.' 'No? Really?' 'Of course not.' 'But stay until when?' He shrugged. 'That's for you to know, till you feel better, at least.' I looked around rather suspiciously. It didn't look like a bachelor's flat, everything was really tidy. 'Don't you live with anyone? You seem like you should be married.' 'No,' he answered. 'But you don't go out much at night?' 'When I feel like it, I do. You're like an interrogator. Go on, sleep a bit more. Do you want an aspirin?'

"I looked at him closely for the first time and he looked really nice, the furthest thing in the world from the men I think of as the kind who drive you crazy; you could see from a mile away that we were like night and day, yet he was gathering up my troubles and offering me shelter. It was so obvious that it made me mistrustful. I'd never seen such behaviour in a film, unless it was made clear from the beginning that the man was a sadist – but the ones who played that part were usually better looking, super gorgeous, often sombre. Or a priest who collected lost souls. Tomás doesn't like it when I remind him now, but I asked him if he was gay, because I was suffering a horrible attack of curiosity, you know? I needed to take stock of the situation, despite the fact that I had absolutely no desire to sleep with him at that moment. And he said to me, firmly: 'We'll clear that up if you stay till tomorrow, OK? Now, I'm going to finish this design.'

"And when I, disorientated, mumbled 'I don't understand you', he took me back over to the sofa, covered me up with a blanket and smiled: 'It's people like me I don't understand,' he said. 'Good night.'"

XIV

Airborne Seeds

If one wants to be able to visit a memory, according to widely held belief, it's advisable to cultivate it beforehand. There are people who dedicate a lot of time and care to this act of cultivation, polishing the golden letters on the tombstones of their dead in the belief that if they don't do it often and methodically enough, the dead will no longer even have names. These are opinions, sums that don't come out the same for everyone. In horror stories the terrifying apparition or echo of a name pursues those who've denied the shades and fled from the past, which grips them in the dead of night. There are those who don't trust literature, of course, but I take that to be an oversight.

Those of us who, like Edith Piaf, boast of lighting the fire of survival with our memories and of being unafraid of them, are often scorched, as clumsy in pyromania as in the cultivation of memory. Memory gets cross with those who practise it clandestinely and use slapdash techniques. But time, like the rain, falls ineluctably on all gardens, and the moment will always come when something appears. Even on the façade of a Romanesque church empty of worshippers, locked and bolted, we see a little tree growing up between the stones, and who knows where it's come from or who it commemorates. But there it is.

Unlike other crops, these seeds of memory spend long spells floating in the air, and we hear them buzzing like insects, the sound of a bad omen for those who would escape them. Sometimes we catch one and let it go again, almost frightening it, but now our awakened senses can't help but follow its route until we see it lose altitude and come to rest. Then we appear, though perhaps by stealth, to fertilise the dry earth fate chose for its brief rest, we mark the site with a sign, cherishing the hope that it might return and put down roots. And if it doesn't come back, bad news: the almond trees get hit by frost after they've blossomed, that's how we think of it. We are becoming, whether we accept it or not, the nurturers of that memory.

This is all very strange. And metaphors are to blame. When they have me cornered they do with me what they will, I see what isn't there and I can't see what is. Maybe Magda's right, I should write poems. Sometimes we force a vocation on ourselves that isn't there, while others resist the call of the muses. Rosario Tena is sure she was born to paint, she's burned all her bridges in the attempt, and she's never been better than mediocre. I wonder if she knows, if my mother ever told her. On the other hand, her talent for teaching is truly extraordinary, no-one had managed to inject me with a passion for learning until I met her.

I thought about this that afternoon as soon as I'd said goodbye to Magda, after refusing, though gently, her offer of a lift when she discovered I didn't have my car. "Talking to you has stirred up all kinds of things inside me," I told her, "don't take it the wrong way, but I'd rather walk home, I need a good long walk on my own." I thanked her for not insisting and she thanked me for telling her such lovely stories. "And I don't mean the ones about Don Luis and his cohorts," she said with a smile. We'd ended up talking for a while about the strange adventures of 18th-century travellers, all of them of quite extravagant *tarannà*, of how difficult it was to imagine, in an age of mobile phones and helicopters and faxes, the inconveniences their peregrinations must have entailed, the bravery. "Because when you read the documents," I told Magda, "no sooner are they in Trinidad, than they're in Jamaica, London, Cádiz or Las Rozas, and the first thing that comes into my mind is where would they relieve themselves, what would their luggage be like, their clothes, their means of travel by sea or land, their friends left behind; they never write about those things in their letters, and of course, you clutch at that little box with the portrait of a woman inside like it's your last hope, Carlota Picolet, what a beautiful name, don't you think? Was she fair or dark?" "How silly your curiosity is!" said Magda, "with the number of forgotten family photos you must have lying around in drawers." And that phrase stuck with me for days.

We kissed each other goodbye, realising we'd become friends. "Take care of yourself," she said, "and think about what you've got, I have fewer resources than you and I'm more alone. In this vale of tears, happy are those who can have a good time once in a while, don't you think it's a privilege to have someone to argue with, to laugh with, someone to caress and wait for? Your husband must be an angel."

And thinking of that vale of tears, I seemed to see them fall from the sky as if the inhabitants of the world beyond were crying over our evasive memories. As soon as I left Magda I became embroiled in the gardens of memories and airborne seeds, lost in the woods of metaphor, a blissful vice. But I wasn't afraid, I advanced as if to the rhythm of an anthem. The clouds of fear had been swept away and the sun filtered through the clearings in the woods.

I was tired when I got home, because between one thing and another I'd walked several kilometres, and after a couple of bowls of an exquisite gazpacho that trusty Remedios had left for me in the fridge, I went into the clean bedroom, aware that my conscience was calm. There were no messages on the answering machine. I lay down on the bed, which for the last several weeks had been a torture rack, and began to think about how horrible it would be if Tomás left me. I looked at the clock; at 10 p.m. I'd phone him and tell him that the people from Panasonic hadn't come but it didn't matter any more, the bedroom was transformed, it had turned into an open, ventilated space filled with airborne seeds. I'd say pretty, provocative, spirited things to him, whatever came out; that I'd redecorated and was inviting him to come and see me. He'd be puzzled. He'd tell me I was crazy but I'd make sure he knew how much I was missing him. And I savoured our conversation in advance, even outlined a few sentences, although I knew rehearsals of this kind were futile.

The room smelled nice. Remedios must have bought a new brand of air freshener. But no, how silly! That's not what it smelled of, but of an enchanted garden whose exotic plants disguised themselves with normal appearances: the fruits of memory. "Because you've been sleeping in this room for quite a while now," I said to myself, "leaving traces, you didn't notice till today," and my eyes slid slowly, delightedly, over familiar objects and furniture, recalling digressions that remained fixed to certain surfaces, a stain on the ceiling, plugs, drawers, books, light sparkling off the mirror, the phone. I was exploring all that domestic vegetation bit by bit, breathing the air as if trying to locate where each different smell came from, to find its hidden fruits, with a certain investigative willingness to go beyond my intoxication with the aromas and attempt to classify them as well. And that's how the blue portrait appeared.

"Not everything can be understood!" I said to Tomás when I brought my mother's self-portrait over from the garret and asked permission to hang it in what was becoming our sitting room.

"I never said it could," he answered in surprise. "And I wasn't trying to explore your soul. I'm not curious, you said so yourself not so long ago, I don't like getting into this kind of conversation. Does it appeal to you that I'm not curious or do you think it a fault? That's what I don't know, it's hard to tell with you."

We'd been together for a month. I think it was his first attempt to put me in front of a mirror and suggest I take off one of my masks. I had, in fact, only recently been praising his discretion, his disinclination to delve into the lives of others. "People don't interest you very much, do they?" I'd asked, expecting him to deny it, to say, "Not always, but your life interests me a great deal, no matter how much you tell me, it seems so little." But he didn't, and things got confused. I remember that brief chat, in which I nearly slipped on the banana peel of my sophistry, because I began to feel exposed, as I had so many times under my mother's impassive gaze.

The portrait, in sepias and blues, was leaning against a bookcase; the previous afternoon I'd gone to the garret for the last time to get it and a few other belongings. I was leaving almost everything for the next tenants. I was cutting my losses – or that's what I believed – considering that phase of my life to be over, although my nervousness at descending those stairs for the last time and going out on to the street, having given the porter the key I'd felt for so often at the bottom of my bag, carried such a charge of old fears that I warned myself to be careful. And I hate warnings like that.

I wandered through the neighbourhood, having a drink in every bar, I passed by the building where Doña Mila, my old Russian teacher, lived and was tempted to go up and see her, but I frightened myself with the thought that she might have died. I'd never appreciated the advantages of that neighbourhood, which I was suddenly missing in the way you mourn what you have squandered. If Doña Mila had appeared and called me by name, I wouldn't have known what to say to her, it would have been like finding myself face to face with a ghost. I quickened my pace. The waiters knew me in the three or four bars where I ended up and weren't surprised to see me with my bundles. I didn't tell them I was making my farewell rounds. They'd seen me before taking things home from skips, "seekers of pearls among the dregs" were common in that part of Antón Martín. I was very careful with the painting, it was a clue that was difficult to hide and might arouse suspicion, so I turned it around and leaned it against the bar, shielding it with my body. And I began to piece together the script for a mystery movie, that's how alcohol always affects me. First sequence: Young woman entering bar with a few bundles, among them a painting, perhaps stolen, that she tries to hide. They know her in the bar. Apprehensive gestures. Someone is staring at her from the other end of the bar. The girl gulps her drink and announces defiantly: "I never look back!" And so on. It was spring, nine o'clock in the evening. I stopped in time, because I didn't want to get drunk. Since I'd moved in with Tomás, I hadn't needed to go back to drinking.

Anyway, I arrived back at my new hideout, no longer so temporary, in a state of wavering euphoria and with an unquenched thirst. I had no desire to think about anything dangerous, I left the bundles on the balcony and when Tomás came home I asked him to take me dancing. I don't know that he came along willingly. He chose the place, a slightly upmarket club near Castellana. He asked me what we were celebrating and I told him the erasing of traces of the past. "Well, that calls for champagne," he said, and ordered some. He's a good dancer but we were somewhat on the defensive. Or at least I was. It annoyed me not to know whether Tomás had noticed that my body was demanding alcohol in order to allay my fears. I told him several times, for no particular reason: "I never look back, let's get that clear." "OK, but watch where you're going, would you?" I was about to get angry because it sounded like a reproach, but understood a second later that he was referring to the fact that I'd just trodden on his foot. And we laughed in each other's arms there in the middle of the dance floor.

The next afternoon, however, looking at the portrait of my mother leaning against the bookshelf, that phrase, "watch where you're going" rose up to my mouth with the bad flavour of an undigested meal. Mum and Tomás weren't joining forces to give me that warning, were they? Well no, as a matter of fact, it's not my style to watch where I'm going, but so what? Is it so difficult to accept me as I am? If I get myself into scrapes, I'll get out of them on my own. And I felt like screaming, "Two against one! Not fair! I'm getting out of this house!"

But the rawness left from my relationship with Roque had taught me, if nothing else, to abhor hysteria. I looked away from the portrait. Tomás seemed to be waiting for me to say something.

"OK, agreed," I said, "you're not curious. Nevertheless (I'm telling you because I can see it) you're looking at me with eyes of an inquisitor. What are you thinking?"

He was silent for a moment, then said, "I'm thinking about you. Something's up with you and maybe you don't even realise it. It's starting to seem as though . . . look, I don't know, what does it matter! These psychological soundings bore me, I swear. And anyway, I'm in a hurry."

"It's starting to seem like what? Say whatever it is!"

"As though you provoke questions, you're wanting me to ask you things, begging almost. And then you get angry if I comply. Anyway, in my profession we flee from approximations. I know that's a crude summary of the situation."

It wasn't a crude summary at all, I thought as I looked back to the portrait. The same thing happened to me with her. I liked to boast to my friends that I had a mother who was neither cloying nor controlling, but there was nothing I craved more than her questions and the malign pleasure of leaving them unanswered. The truth is that she had come to ask me fewer and fewer. Without casting back any further, just the previous afternoon . . . But no, I didn't want to remember the previous afternoon.

Tomás stood up and bent over to give me a kiss. "Sorry if I was a little sharp. You know I've got an urgent appointment. Of course, hang your mother's portrait wherever you want. But don't play tricks on yourself. That's what I meant."

"Tricks? What do you mean by that? Give me an example!"

"Well, when you say not everything can be understood. Unimportant things can't be understood because you don't try. But if it matters to you, if you're obsessed by something, it's worth making an effort to understand yourself a bit better. It's not that difficult either."

"Would you mind telling me what you're referring to?"

He'd already taken a few steps towards the door and turned around to indicate the painting with his chin.

"Her," he said. "You're always saying you don't love her, that the two of you can do without each other, but you can't hide your passion."

They were looking at each other. In that portrait my mother is about 30 years old; she still is, embalmed there in sepias and blues, with dark penetrating eyes. Was Tomás the kind of man she would have liked at that age, when I was eight? I was jealous but I turned it around, I'm an expert at this type of interior alchemy. I stood up and embraced Tomás.

"Jealous?" I whispered in his ear.

"Enough! Don't be silly. See you later."

When Tomás left, I suffered an attack of fury against the painting and began looking for a cupboard in which to put it, I needed to dump it like a corpse. I wasn't yet totally at home in the flat, but I'd seen a storage cupboard above a closet containing cleaning things just next to the kitchen. It was very deep and half-empty. I found a ladder and as I took the painting up tears of rage spilled down my face. Badly hidden injuries, when they resurface, add poison to their bitterness, this was an overdue rage that had begun to grow the previous afternoon when I'd gone to get the painting from the garret. Going into the garret had been terrible enough.

Any move, even for those not overly attached to objects, is itself hard, not only for what you have to throw out, but for what, on similar occasions, you have already discarded. Dead weight. Don't look back. But your hands tremble.

Mine had trembled as I'd taken the painting from the wall, because I started to imagine when and for whom it would turn into a useless piece of junk. Wouldn't it be better for such a judgement to come directly from me? My mother's signature was beginning to be worth something. "Why don't you sell it?" a voice inside me whispered. But I knew I'd never be able to. Hanging it in that garret, while it still harboured none of my memories, had meant taking possession, like marking out a patch of wasteland that was going to need a lot of care and effort before anything could be grown there. Now I was taking leave of what I'd overcome in that place, day by day. And I was also taking leave of the girl, five years younger, who'd stood in the doorway with her suitcases, looking at that empty, inhospitable space for the first time, and wondering, "Can I do this?" while her raging dreams of independence contracted and she perceived strange noises and smells coming from the courtyard through a window that took a long time to close properly.

Little by little, the garret smelled successively of Titanlux paint, sandalwood, coffee, hash and Álvaro Gómez cologne, until Roque arrived and mingled his unmistakable scent with all of mine.

His conquest of territory didn't cooperate with mine, we superimposed on and displaced each other; that was our game, a display of ingenuity, playfulness and pleasure that gradually ate away at us, demolishing possible harvests. I wonder now if I really loved Roque, or if I was just aroused by the fencing exercises, and grew too fond of drinks that had to have their doses increased continually, prepared for each by the other and swallowed greedily. It was a sort of bet, we waited to see who would be the first to run out of energy and credibility, broken against the dawn in that room with blue walls.

And then after a while Roque stopped coming and the garret smelled of his absence, which flourished in all the cracks, a strident and persistent odour which added lyrics to my need for survival, "in-between-rock of living with severed sorrows, rock of survival". Later I brought different rhizomorphs back to the garret to bolster my ego, chipped and flaking as it was, poor thing, and it began to stink of rotten flowers. The idea of death often haunted me, as did the contemplation of how strange it was to live. This whole long and broken story, with sparks of fire and shadowy hollows, had been witnessed by the portrait I now took down with a hammering heart. My grief at moving tugged at what I'd felt as I'd first arrived and the two sensations buried Roque, contained him.

And then, just as I'd taken down the painting and my hands had stopped shaking, the telephone rang, startling me. It was my mother.

"You caught me by a miracle," I told her. "I've just come to pick up a few things. Did you get my letter?"

"Yes, but you didn't tell me where you've moved to, so I've kept ringing you there just in case. How are you?"

"Fine. I've moved up a bit in the world. Did you want something?"

"To know how you are. How have you moved up in the world?"

"Well, the flat where I live now has a lift and no cockroaches and it's bigger. Although, it's hard to give you an idea since you've never been to this one."

"You've never invited me."

"That's true. Besides, it doesn't matter. We should get together for lunch one of these days. Are you going to be in Madrid for a while?"

"No, next week I've got an exhibition in Barcelona. By the way, I wanted to ask you a favour."

"Name it."

"Could you lend me my self-portrait for about a month? I could send someone to pick it up. Would you mind?"

Tears of rage ran down my cheeks. That was all she'd phoned for. She couldn't care less whether I was fine or not, if it had been hard or easy to decide to leave the garret, and before that her house, and wherever else I might leave. Her image, there in front of me, was blurring; the paint was running and the sepia was discolouring the blue.

"You've still got that painting, haven't you?" she said, responding to my silence.

I wiped away the tears with my sleeve. "Well, you see . . . I had it . . ."

"What do you mean, you had it?"

"Yeah, Mum, I'm sorry. I'd rather not have had to tell you, but I ran into a lot of problems and I sold it, I had no other way out."

There was a silence. I was sure we were both seeing the same thing: a narrow, deserted street in Tangier. I'd have bet anything. A nameless street.

"Did you look for any other way out?" she asked at last.

"One or two. It occurred to me, for example, to call you, but I didn't fancy it. I know I did wrong, that's life. After all, the painting was mine. And that's that."

She received the blow with her typical sangfroid, and asked if I knew who had the picture now. I said no, that I'd sold it in the Rastro and it wasn't there any more. Well, she said, what can we do? She added that she hadn't imagined things had been going so badly for me, "don't worry, not that bad, occasional rough patches, now I'm studying like mad for my exams," she wished me luck and I her, and as a finishing touch, the usual "keep in touch, take care". I don't remember if we talked about Rosario, I don't think so. I was anxious to hang up.

I'd needed her to tell me off. I needed it so badly.

Memories branch out in unexpected profusion, they resemble the twists and turns of an unplanned journey, it's difficult to resist the temptation to explore them, and even harder not to get lost, to return to the source that unites them and from which they flow. Having control over the adventure is a rare privilege, and that evening, after my conversation with Magda, I experienced it. I went back through time, as though visiting different levels of a spacious greenhouse to check the effect of the climate on each floor. The climate was my mother, the sun coming back out from behind the clouds, and the greenhouse was my house, Tomás's and mine, our house. Or perhaps it was the reverse, she was the flower in the greenhouse that needed my warmth, in order for me to evoke her and keep her in the land of the living. A myriad of metaphors occurred to me, leaping one on top of the other, while I lay on the bed and waited till I could phone Cazorla at 10 p.m., a pleasant and entertaining wait without any tension.

The memories revolved around a portrait hidden in that very home, but in summoning them I divested them of venom; they acquired the nostalgia of a blues song, not for nothing did they come from a painting in which those tones predominated.

Temptation began to haunt me: if I looked at the picture now, what would happen? I needed to know. At some point I stood up and went to look for it in the high cupboard by the kitchen where it had been stashed for so long. I got out the ladder and climbed up. The picture was under a couple of suitcases, I recognised it by touch, because I'd felt it there before, way at the back.

I had to climb halfway into the cupboard to grasp it. And before I pulled it out I thought: "What if her face is wrinkled and frowning terribly like the picture of Dorian Gray?" But no, the opposite was the case. Although she seemed the same then, later, when I looked more closely, I realised that her dark eyes had stopped looking inward and that her typical pose, head tilted slightly to the right after one of her heavy sighs, now suggested a blend of abandonment, tenderness and an appeal for help.

When I had been seven, we'd spent a month in Tangiers, staying in the house of some friends of my father's, two men with a dog, the older one was a writer. I don't know why we went there. One afternoon my mother took me out for a walk and we bought things in a street full of bazaars. She didn't talk much and I think she was sad in a way that made her indifferent to everything. She sighed several times. "Why do people sigh?" I asked her. Before answering she sighed again. "It can be out of sorrow, or impatience or fear. Sometimes out of relief." But she didn't look at me as she spoke and I understood she didn't want more questions; and also that it wasn't out of relief that she was sighing.

On the way back we were tired of walking, but it was a deserted part of the city, there weren't any cars and suddenly she said she thought we were lost. She was walking more and more slowly, looking around, and the pressure of her hand in mine got weaker until she murmured, "I can't," and she stopped and grabbed the handrail of some stairs. For me, Tangiers is that stairwell, even though if I went back there I don't think I'd be able to find it, certainly not if I looked for it, something, of course, I have no intention of doing. A few days before Dad had told me that at the end of autumn I was going to have a baby brother or sister, a child who never came to be born; it was spring and I blamed my mother's fainting spell on that capricious and perverse baby who had climbed up from her belly to squeeze her throat and prevent her from breathing. I already knew that women carried their children inside their bodies for a while, but I imagined them fully formed from the first day except smaller, and that they grew in size as well as in badness or goodness. My little brother, although minuscule, was bad and he envied me. Mum had slid down holding on to the handrail, had sat or fallen on to one of the steps, and had closed her eyes. I picked up the bag and parcels she'd dropped, then I knelt down and started giving her little kisses and calling her by her name, but she didn't answer. She was leaning against the railing and her face was very cold. So were her hands. I didn't know what to do, but I was sure that if I began to cry all would be lost, because she had told me many times that in moments of real danger the worst thing to do was cry, and besides I knew this from stories. I also knew that I couldn't leave her because I was protecting her, that was my rôle. I have never known with such certainty that I was exactly where I needed to be as I did on that afternoon in Tangiers, beside my unconscious mother who had only me to rely on, on my faith in fate. And so I turned my fear into hope, and at the end of the narrow, deserted street there appeared the silhouette of a little man in a striped djellabah and a red fez who walked slowly towards us. I waved for him to come over and he hurried to us. "Help me, please, my mother's not very well." He understood Spanish, although he spoke it strangely. He was just the kind of mysterious, calm and wise being you need on an occasion like that, I knew it as soon as he bent over and began to give Mum's face gentle little slaps and recite something in Arabic that sounded like a prayer. When she opened her eyes, which was almost immediately, he made her sniff a little vial he took out of his djellabah. Mum sighed deeply, this time out of relief, and smiled with her head on one side like it is in the painting, while she stretched out her hands in search of mine. The tiny man took us to find a taxi and wouldn't hear of accepting a tip. "Your daughter is much courageous," he said in farewell.

The next day, in an upstairs room of that strange house we were staying in, Mum began to paint her self-portrait. "Use lots of blues," I told her, "because when you fainted everything was blue."

I cleaned the dust off the painting, took it to the bedroom and lay back down on the bed without taking my eyes off it. It's not very big. I remembered how she'd finished it back in Madrid on my birthday. She'd stayed up late several nights in a row to finish it in time to give it to me on that day.

"Are you lending it to me?" I asked her, when she came in with it to wish me a happy birthday.

"No. It's yours, yours, forever. You can have it in your room forever."

"Forever? Even if I go to other rooms when I'm big?"

"Of course. Forever is forever."

I turned eight years old that 11th of June, and the word *forever* was the wrapping on the present, I felt as though it was encased in silk paper that wouldn't ever wrinkle.

Well, I sighed with relief, despite my neglect, Mum had not aged like Dorian Gray or the woman in my dream who was being mistreated by a gigolo. So many images, so many words, so many rooms, so many forevers flowing into now, bringing our house to life! I went out to water the plants on the balcony. It had cooled down.

At 10 p.m. on the dot I phoned Tomás and had the good fortune to find him in, and sounding energetic. Everything was going well, he'd been about to phone me at that very moment and he was dying to see me. I told him he was the man of my dreams and that I was waiting for him in a new home, mine, full of exotic flowers. The thing surfaced about the airborne seeds that alight in drawers and shelter in armchairs, and I knew he was enjoying listening to me, although he told me I was getting madder by the day, it was clear from the way he pronounced the word *mad*, quite frequent in our conversations. I feel it as a caress or a sombre warning, according to which part of his soul it comes from, that night it tasted of a champagne cocktail, as did everything we said to one another.

"Have you picked up a girlfriend down there? I want the truth."

I'd never asked him anything like this, never mind seriously, and I heard a pleased laugh, and once again, he told me that I was mad.

"Look here, I might be going a little bit mad, but it's because it's been such a long time since we've spoken, too many days without hearing your voice, an eternity."

And then Tomás said something very surprising: "I'm flattered to hear it seems like an eternity to you, sweetheart, but the facts contradict your exaggeration. It's been two days."

"Two days? Can't be."

"Less three hours, to be precise, because it was late the night before last when you woke me up to tell me about the phantoms of the world beyond and Robert De Niro as a cemetery guard . . ."

"It wasn't a cemetery . . ."

"OK, whatever. By the way, that scene where De Niro eats a hard-boiled egg is from *Angel Heart*, I've seen a lot of movies too. Then you went slightly Dostoyevsky, don't you remember?"

Yes, of course I remembered, but it couldn't be that only two nights had passed since then, but yes, he said, he was absolutely sure because it so happens . . . I stopped listening and did some mental calculations, from the night at the Residuo to the one in the Indian settlement was one, and from then to now was two. It was true, it added up.

"Hey, you're right, it was the night before last, I just thought about it. And yet that seems incredible, I swear."

"Why?"

"Well, you'll see, a lot of things have happened to me, so many, you can't imagine."

"Am I allowed to ask if you've picked up a boyfriend?"

"I don't need one, I'm just waiting for you, I've done up the flat to welcome you and it smells of flowers. It's interior things that have been happening."

He started to laugh.

"Interior? How dangerous! Well, tie them up with little coloured ribbons so they don't fly away."

"That's what I've been doing all evening. I love you. When are you coming home?"

"I don't think it'll be more than a couple days, certainly no more than three. We're nearly finished here."

"Really? That's great!"

"But I hope they don't stretch out as long as the last two did, because I won't be able to find my way around your interior gardens. You'll have to hire me a guide. And, please, can you find someone less sinister than Robert De Niro to do the job? Look in the yellow pages. Maybe under the word *love*."

"I love it when you get surreal. And you've got a gorgeous voice. Has anyone ever told you that?"

"You haven't, my Cazorla girlfriend has, though, she's a hot little brunette."

By the time we said goodbye, I'd lost all trace of sleepiness and felt clear and sure. Capable of any task. I looked at my mother's portrait.

"Know what?" I said to her, "I think I'm going to go see Rosario. If she's not there, I'll just come home. It's not so late."

XV

The Lecturer with the Granny Glasses

She came in November, to cover for the head of department, who was on sick leave, a guest lecturer I think they called her – "they're going to send us someone who's got clout with Don Carlos," I overheard some classmates saying in the bar, after we'd missed more than a week of classes – it was the kind of post people accepted in conditions of extreme poverty. She hadn't written her doctoral thesis and wasn't sure if she wanted to take the exams in order to dedicate herself entirely to teaching, but she was enthusiastic about the painting of the Italian *trecento*, which was what she taught us, although there were other subjects on the syllabus too.

"OK, I'm going to start with the *dolce stil nuovo*, some of those artists such as Orcagna, Giotto or Ambrogio Lorenzetti began the 14th century already in their creative primes, and I'll try, though it's a bit of a leap, to get as far as Leonardo da Vinci, who died in 1516, unless our voyage is interrupted, because I probably won't be with you for the whole course," she told us on the first day. "So you'll have to let me tell you things in my own way and not in strict chronological order, you can imagine, if you want, that we're going out on a field trip.

"The *trecento* is not a closed corral, its roof and floor are open, in other words the trajectories of artists who lived, died or were born during the 14th century intersect, they start in the previous century or run into the next, they meet or at least hear each other spoken of at some point, they're influenced by Dante and Petrarch, who would also have seen some of their pictures, and they are dependent on different families of magnates, families with ties of blood, marriage or antagonism between them, whose villainies shouldn't make us forget the fruits of their patronage. It all overlaps, it's a period of ferment, of stories that flow ceaselessly and ceaselessly mix their waters. So, given the difficulties of classification and the short space of time I'm going to have – as we all hope Don Carlos will be back soon – I've decided to go through the paintings by theme rather than dates, and to put special emphasis on the ones I like best, I'm sorry. You'll have to take it like a collection of samples, like a portion, open to amplification, since everything is a portion of something. I should warn you now that I get overwhelmed by totalities, and I can't conceive of knowledge in any other way than as fragmentary. But, if I can get you to look at the few paintings I want to introduce you to with even a tenth of the enthusiasm they excite in me, I'll be more than satisfied. By the way, my name is Rosario Tena and I'm 31 years old. Could one of you go and call the porter to see if the projector is working properly?"

It was not a terribly orthodox introductory speech, and despite the indifference and suspicion that generally greet a substitute teacher in a large lecture hall, there was an almost immediate silence.

She was slight, with straight hair, wore frameless little granny glasses and a beret. She hadn't spoken very loudly, or made any gesture that indicated a desire to make an impression, but rather had that conviction some timid people have, as if they are tossing bold seeds into the air without expecting to see them settle. I was in the second row, next to the aisle.

"Thank you, Señorita . . ." she said as she saw me stand up to go and find the porter.

I have quite a good ear for intonations, and the third word sounded like a question.

"Soler," I said. "Águeda Soler."

And we looked at each other.

We'd already looked at each other earlier in the faculty bar, glances in which I perceived that my own appearance had startled her as much as hers had me. I was struck by her pallor, by the very long, black coat she was wearing, and by the way she sat with her body arched slightly against the back of the chair. She had her hands crossed behind her head, and was muttering something as she looked off into the distance, seemingly absorbed. "I wonder if that's the Art History substitute," I said to myself, noticing that next to her empty coffee cup she had our text book open and some slides on top of it, which she checked once in a while. I must have aroused her curiosity too, I was thinking and biting a fingernail, this used to be an unconscious thing, later it became less so, in photos I look interesting when I'm biting a fingernail, I don't know if it was that, but when my eyes wandered in her direction they occasionally met hers. At one moment there was even a hint of a complicit smile when a clumsy fellow spilled Coke all over his notes and had no idea how to clean them off. "Oh no, oh no!" he murmured nervously, "oh no, oh no!" And I fell in love with the almost immediately perceptible intelligence that Rosario's fleeting smile projected, kind and witty, belonging to someone who, without interrupting their own thoughts, at the same time doesn't miss what's going on around them. She stood up, went to the bar and got a cloth, which she handed to the boy. Then she went back and sat down at her table near mine. We were both alone, and no-one approached either of us.

I never made friends with my classmates. I cultivated friends in more downmarket places, and going to the faculty, which I didn't do every day either, was a routine and even somewhat annoying task. If I finished my degree, without much effort nor particular interest, it was simply to please my father, who imagined me as a researcher at some American university.

"I assure you," I told him one day, "that if I tried a little, you could wallpaper your office with my certificates of distinction, but I've got the most boring lecturers, Dad, they're not in the least stimulating, a lot of them only teach at university so they can get political posts later, they give lectures to fulfil the requirements, repeating what you can find in any text book, and the lecture halls are huge, no-one goes. People want to write a brilliant exam answer to impress a lecturer, don't they? Because you like what they say or they've fired up your imagination. Isn't that what happened when you met Mum?" He said yes, I was right, and we ended up talking about *The Rebellion of the Masses*, an essay he's always liked; well, I don't know if he has time to read anything these days. Anyway, my father owes the only distinction I received in the entire time I spent at university to Rosario Tena, though she, let go as she was after Easter break, wasn't the one to grant it, but rather an ailing and downcast Don Carlos, who'd had a kidney and perhaps something more removed, though certainly not his critical faculties. I haven't much to boast about in the way of a c.v., but I completed that exam with a flourish. I'd like to have half the inspiration to tell the story of Vidal y Villalba, the essay was ordered and rigorous but went off on all sorts of tangents. The question was about Leonardo da Vinci, and I covered all the things I knew about him, and I still know them because what you learn well you never lose, I'd even read his complete diaries and I headed the exercise with a phrase of his that I'd had pinned up in the blue-papered garret for ages: "It is useful for the artist to go over in his mind at night the things he has learned or studied during the day. In bed, in the quiet nocturnal hours, it is good to trace in the imagination the shapes of figures that require more study. Then the images of the objects come to life and the impression becomes stronger and more permanent." – What a brilliant man! And he'd invented machines as well. That was why Roque's mocking comments about the Mona Lisa annoyed me later.

But, my God, will it ever be possible for me to manage to relive one isolated incident from my life without so many more of my own or other people's coming out entangled with it, can I ever catch a lost fish that doesn't drag up family and see the sun sparkle on its scales?

What happens to me is a kind of illness, and if I found Rosario's very special classes so fascinating it was because I knew from the first day that she, as an intermediary between our chaotic *fin de millennium* and the painting of the *trecento*, was touched by the same disease. Or to put it another way, in speaking about classifying paintings by emotions, sensuality and horror, harmony and disorder, effort and apathy, hell and heaven, she was tearing off strips from other secret parts of her soul, I didn't know more than this, because it was a while before we became friends, but I was certain, these things you notice by looking at each other, the same way a homosexual or a drug addict recognises another one at first glance. The lecturer with the granny glasses belonged to the ontological species of bird, or at least that's how I catalogued her then.

Once reassured, with the help of the porter, that the projector was in perfect working order, Rosario Tena carefully wrote a date, 13 September 1321, on the blackboard, in large clear letters.

"I've already told you," she said as she turned back to face us, "that I'm not a slave to dates, but this one's important: it is that of the death, in Ravenna, at the age of 56, of Dante Alighieri."

Then she asked if any of us had read *The Divine Comedy* and not a single hand was raised. She understood, she said. "You get frightened by it as with all the classics they try and inject into our veins from early childhood, but *The Divine Comedy* is no harder to read than Joyce's *Ulysses*, for example, and quite a bit more fun.

"But questions of taste aside," she said, "if I mention it, it's because I think *The Divine Comedy* is a fundamental text for anyone who wants to learn to look at a painting and decipher its symbols, it stimulates the comprehension of the chaotic. There's a fantastic translation by Ángel Crespo."

She began to talk about *The Divine Comedy*, and I realised I was taking notes, strange for me, as if I was taking photographs. A she-wolf, a panther and a lion appear successively at the foot of a hill. Then Virgil comes out, a kind of shadow who starts to speak. And I was seeing it, and ready to follow wherever it led, the voice of that girl in the granny glasses only eight years older than me and four years younger than the perplexed Dante when he paused in the dark forest at the beginning and confessed he'd lost his way. She didn't refer to a book as she told us about it, "superficially", as she said, but all the while inserting quotes from memory, as if flying over the text halfway between sure and naïve. And from the dark forest where the poet finds himself lost, not knowing how he got there, Virgil guided Dante, and Rosario Tena guided me, first through an immense and terrible chasm in the centre of the earth and later up a path on a mountain formed by the rocks Lucifer displaced in his fall, arriving at last, having cleared seven precipices, at the longed for summit of the gardens of Eden where the poet encountered Beatrice, who looked at the sun with the eyes of an eagle and said to him:

> You make yourself so dense with wealth
> Of false imagination, and cannot see
> All that you would if you had freed yourself.

It is a transparent world but at the same time difficult to understand because it catches us off guard, because we're accustomed to evil; a somewhat cold space, perhaps, like the sharp exercise of intelligence, but as Dantean in its terrors as the one we're accustomed to describing as his; how dearly we pay for the sublimation of the dark and tortuous, the literary excursion by way of the lion's mouth. And next to me a skinny boy with deep-set eyes who usually slept through every class breathed deeply and then, with a sort of huff, said, "Wow," as if to himself, "she sure knows her stuff, this one!"

It wasn't only caves, underground rivers, beings twisted in torment and sinister lagoons that Virgil and Rosario showed us, but also the cold wind felt when emerging into the light from below, a distant and vast light of stars that pulsate in another hemisphere, sending us their rays of hope. But they're pauses, and we need to know that their essence resides in their very transience, pain is there, behind any crag with open jaws, and that mustn't be forgotten, Dante won't let us forget it. In Paradise he never stops making references to our mortal condition, in the same way as we find patches of pleasure in Hell and Purgatory; that's what the coded message consists of, it makes us notice how during the course of the odyssey he gradually reveals the complementary aspects of the frieze of life and death, of horror and blessedness, of the near and the distant. *The Divine Comedy* was that most of all, a travel book with illustrations. And she, Rosario Tena, our Virgil, saw in those illustrations the adventures of a man able to sharpen his intelligence and overcome his cowardice to search out salvation in the bosom of chaos; and I took notes so feverishly that my hand hurt, because things were occurring to me constantly at the edge of what she was saying, the examples she was giving.

"For example, Virgil makes Dante understand, at the end of the first part, that to escape from the Inferno he has no choice but to depend on the devil, to let himself fall down his enormous hairy flank, and thus they both start to slide as if descending a staircase, down the strands of the devil's hair. At a certain moment, Dante realises in terror that he's going up instead of down and thinks he's returning to the realm of shadows, but it was no trick of the devil, nor had he fallen when he fell furthest, on the contrary, they were going up simply because they were on their way out: 'To another hemisphere you now have access,' Virgil tells him. Don't you think it's exciting to escape from evil up the very stairs of evil, managing to change its direction without denying its existence, taking advantage of it?"

More than a quarter of an hour had gone by and total silence reigned in the lecture hall. It was November, we'd just had three days off for All Saints' Day and Rosario Tena said that the fresco she was about to show us seemed particularly apt to commemorate the faithful dead.

"Because we live in the suburbs of death," she said, "and only when we've perceived that can we understand works like those of Orcagna."

She said this in a serious, quiet voice. Quite a while later I found out that around that time, she'd lost a brother in a motorbike accident.

"We are frequently going to find ourselves encountering themes from *The Divine Comedy* in the paintings I will introduce to you, ascent and fall, elevation and abyss, fear and courage, and always the threat of death circling life like an invisible entourage. Or the opposite, because at other times it will be the troops of life who assault the castle of death and cause its phantoms to flee. So," Rosario concluded, "the painters of the *trecento* had read Dante like a breviary and Giotto, for example, was also a close friend of his. They're artists who are as literary as *The Divine Comedy* can be pictorial. We sometimes might even think we lack some little inscription, like a caption to a cartoon. We'll soon see one."

She proceeded to show us some frescos from the Composanto in Pisa attributed to Orcagna, a painter I'd never heard of before. The slide show took up the rest of the class, and she restricted herself to brief commentaries, amplifying significant and insignificant details, as if exploring one by one all the corners of a room. All very slowly, so it would stay fixed on our retinas, which is what – she said – the pleasure of contemplation entails.

At one end of the fresco you could see a group of ladies and gentlemen relaxing in an orchard to the sound of a clavichord. Two angels above them held a sign, unfurled like a tapestry, which read: *Neither much knowledge nor wealth, and much less vanity or ancient nobility, will liberate these people from death*, in Italian, of course, but she translated it. On the other side, a mounted procession, also of ladies and gentlemen, advanced unconcerned, along a mountainside, and was surprised to discover three open coffins containing decomposing corpses. The whole sky was full of angels and demons who, like a swarm of surreal insects, were fighting over the living. In the wasteland, apart from death's colossal scythe, two hermits, given over to their meditations, seemed to be the only ones with serene faces.

"The painter, if it was Orcagna, which isn't certain," said Rosario Tena, "has put the accent more on the inexplicable and the mysterious than on the depiction of a moralistic theme. I see this painting as a hymn to the absurd, perhaps that's why it seems so modern to me and at the same time so timeless. Since the world began, living and dying have been two sides of the same coin tossed up in the air, but if it comes out heads it's even more absurd. To me, if you want to know the truth, living's the strange thing. See you Friday."

That's how the lecture ended. At the bottom of the notes I'd taken I jotted: "Living's the strange thing. (Possible song title.)"

That evening I started reading *The Divine Comedy*.

XVI

Break with the Maisonette

A lot of things happened that term. Most importantly, I moved out. On the very morning that I first saw the lecturer with the granny glasses in the faculty bar, I was writing a letter to my mother that I never sent; my letter-writing addiction keeps pace with my epistolary repentance, all my books and drawers reveal drafts whose addressees were usually her or Roque, and later Rosario as well, some in sealed and stamped envelopes, others unfinished; and that's not counting all the ones I've torn up.

That one I haven't torn up. It appeared the other day between the pages of *The Divine Comedy* no less, in "Purgatory", and it goes like this:

Dear Mother,

When I told you yesterday that I was moving out, you didn't ask me for an explanation. That's what hurts most, you never ask for explanations, so you force me to give you ones that don't explain, in order to justify conduct of mine that your silence censures. What I said must have surprised you and maybe even offended you, I try not to be seen to be begging at your door for a few tokens of compassion or even anger, and that makes me lie and get confused. I would rather you'd slammed a door, shaking the walls of that sumptuous new maisonette I detest, that's what I didn't tell you yesterday, I'm leaving because I hate it, because you didn't ask for my advice when choosing it or when getting rid of pieces of furniture I was very attached to. You'll say I'm almost impossible to get on with, that I went to Geneva for a month, that I put everything off and I've even asked you to leave me alone on occasion, said it didn't matter to me, that you always make the decisions and I've been grateful, but Mother, the four months I spent there made me miss the smell of our old house desperately, with its traces of disorder and Dad's indecisions. I know you don't like us to talk about him, that you think it's futile, and it is, dredging things up from under the bridge, Dad left us eight years ago, the two of us, alone, face to face with our differences, yes, water under the bridge. I would like, though I'll never be able to ask, to find with you the points of contact that might exist despite our differences, for you to help me accept those differences; it's when you forget them or try to overrule them that the chasm that separates us deepens. And when did that begin? I'd also like to know how I've let you down, I know I'm not easy to get through to and I put up barriers, I can seem inflexible, but you bend as little as I do. Anyway, getting back to the maisonette . . .

I didn't finish the letter. Possibly because I started to entertain myself by watching the lecturer with the granny glasses.

Anyway, getting back to the maisonette (which my mother claimed to have set up for the two of us with such high hopes and in which I stayed for less than five months), it was, and still is, in the district of Bernabeu, spacious and bright, it had three bathrooms, two separate entrances and enough space so that we could live together without having to bother each other. It was taken for granted that I could decorate my part, which was quite a bit smaller, and furnish it in my own style, bring whoever I wanted there, but later I understood that my rejection of it stemmed, almost like a physical repugnance, from the realisation that, faced with so much light and cleanliness, I'd lost my familial traces and didn't have any of my own.

Once Christmas had passed, sweetened by the reading of Dante, I moved to the garret in Antón Martín. There, little by little, first through a staple diet of solitary wandering and later through one of erotic excess, I gradually erased the rupture with my adolescence, when, as an only child, I'd been determined to escape, even if without grace, from the tyranny of my cultured and separated parents, parents who believed they'd raised me to fly with my own wings and not fall into self-pity. I made a living from my Russian translations, read constantly, and my relationship with my mother improved. We met often for meals, and I still kept clothes and books at the maisonette, she'd given me a set of keys, which she never let me return, although I seldom used them. "Even if you're not coming here for the moment," she'd say, "they could come in handy for a friend in trouble, you never know. And that space is yours." She said "for the moment" in a mechanical and unconvincing way, as if pressing a switch that obscured rather than illuminated her words; lies and deterioration tend to sneak in through temporal phrases. I soon guessed that she didn't regard my leaving the maisonette as something temporary. And I think, though I have no proof, that it came as a relief to her.

What is beyond doubt, on the other hand, is that my suspicion of her relief, well-founded or not, hardened my resolve never to return.

The beginning of summer coincided with a streak of effervescence and plenitude, one of those phases when it seems nothing will be impossible. I'd met Roque at the beginning of March, and while he might already have started to become an addiction, nothing had yet made me put up my guard. There'd been no withdrawal symptoms, nor had his behaviour betrayed itself as counterproductive to the cultivation of my own interests, which were more intense and varied each day. On the contrary, I read voraciously, went to museums I'd never visited, wrote songs and submitted my Russian translations more punctually than ever. I needed only a quick shower and a coffee to give me a deer-like agility and clear my head, no matter how late I'd stayed up the night before. Although I hadn't ruled out the idea of sitting the exams for some post, and never even considered the possibility of not passing them, I'd managed to settle into the purest *carpe diem*. And my new abode was growing on me. I was over the worst. Or so I thought.

In my memory of that period, a series of paths spring from the Italian *trecento*, with it at the centre, a profuse, enchanted and sometimes terrible garden; paths that interweave with those travelled by figures from Giotto, Dante, Fra Angelico or Lorenzetti, I still see those paintings reproduced on postcards pinned to the blue walls of the garret, their traces remain, interwoven with my own story, their scents and flavours mix, creating a blend of lust and self-absorption, evil and forgiveness.

"Don't you ever tire of spinning?" Roque would ask me, his eyes black as coal. At other times he'd half-close them, he was sensual and lazy, he fell asleep before me and I can't remember him ever getting up before I did. What often happened was that I'd be woken by him ringing my doorbell at an unreasonable hour because he felt like seeing me, it was ages before he'd accept the extra key I offered every once in a while, "extra keys are locks on the game of love, the more difficulties you take away, the more you create, didn't you know that?" How I loved those maxims then, and he was probably right, as I'd later discover. In the morning I'd take a shower, get dressed, give him a kiss, leave him sleeping and go out, humming some new inter-rock song. It didn't matter if he wasn't there when I came home and hadn't left a note, it was part of a game that had nothing to do with keys, I didn't mind losing track of him for a few days either, he was always going to want me and miss me, I was sure, it was horrible to think that a bird in the hand was worth two in the bush.

I regarded all proverbs as horrible and I loved to display my nonconformist attitude to that entire compendium of popular wisdom. Today it strikes me as an excessively radical position, not all aphorisms are as petty as I then maintained, and besides, I should have been grateful for the metaphorical riches they provided, since they fed – if only through my contradiction of them – the poetic style of some of my songs, like "Bird in the Hand". Another saying I hated, "Jack of all trades, master of none", inspired the lyrics of "Master Jack", an inter-rock song that, although I never recorded it, brought in a bit of money because I sold the rights to some well-known singers. And it became quite famous over that summer, it was played on the radio and in the discos. What I wanted, and what seemed possible then, was to take on the world.

I ran into Rosario Tena one Sunday morning at the beginning of September, in the Reina Sofía Museum. I'd hardly spoken to her while she'd been my lecturer, because neither of us spent much time in the faculty bar, and, no matter how much I like a lecturer, waiting to speak to them after class for no good reason other than to demonstrate my brilliance wasn't something I would ever do. I suppose this refusal to do anything that might smack of sucking up was another thing I inherited from my father. The teacher should approach the student – he'd say – not the other way around. Even so, when Rosario Tena left almost without saying goodbye, I found myself reluctantly, perhaps even guiltily, wishing I'd found the chance to thank her for the lectures.

In other more obscure ways her absence seemed to leave something unfinished between us. It had often seemed as though she was giving her lectures for me alone, but given that she never sought me out or greeted me in any special way, I rejected this impression as false, something my better judgement suggested I ignore, in light of my inclination to egomania.

So, I was very pleased to run into Rosario again that September morning when I didn't have anything exciting planned. It was midday, and my solitary visit to an exhibition of Cubist painting was postponed as soon as I caught sight, through the gallery windows, of that dear familiar figure.

I stood looking at her for a while, unsure whether or not to approach her, because she hadn't seen me, nor did she look as though she had the slightest desire to pay attention to the outside world. Perhaps she was waiting for someone. She was sitting on a stone bench in the internal courtyard with her head hanging and hands fallen limply at her sides. She looked unwell and very pale, as though she hadn't seen a ray of sunshine all summer. Her hair had grown and was pulled back in a ponytail. She didn't move or look around her, nor was she reading.

I walked over and stood in front of her, but it took her a few moments to raise her vacant eyes to mine.

"Remember me?" I asked her. "I was in the Art History class you taught last year, I suppose I don't have to call you Señorita Tena."

She nodded.

"You remember me or you don't mind if I call you Rosario?"

"Both," she said in a flat voice, without the slightest sign of that conscientious, friendly gaze that caught my attention the first time I saw her in the faculty bar.

I asked her if she was waiting for someone, she wasn't, and then if she minded if I sat down with her for a while. She shrugged her shoulders.

"Whatever, it doesn't matter to me. Sorry," she added, "I'm not up to much today. I'm having a really bad day. A horrible day." Her voice broke.

I don't like to pry, but I can't stand anyone crying either, although my usual reaction to another's tears is flight. But that morning, I sat down beside Rosario Tena without a second thought and put my arm around her bony shoulders that began to shake almost immediately. They were bare, and stuck out of a black dress with thin straps, that accentuated the whiteness of her skin.

It didn't seem the right moment to talk about myself, to tell her how much I'd learned from her lectures, and to have come out with a brilliant remark would have been almost a sin. At that moment she was not the inspired lecturer who was able to fly over *The Divine Comedy* with a serene demeanour and diamond flashes in her eyes, she was a tortured soul who writhed in the flames of Hell. And me, what rôle was I to play in that scene?

"If you want to tell me anything, tell me, and if not, no problem. I'm very fond of you, really, and I can see you're in a bad way. I'd like to help you," I said to her, surprising myself with the affection in my voice.

She burst into tears, her head buried in my jacket and we stayed like that for a while, me stroking her shoulders and hair and her crying, until I started to feel awkward, and look around a bit out of the corner of my eye. So I asked her if she'd like to come to my place, which wasn't far away, and she said OK, but without – not then or on the way to the garret – putting aside her mute and even rather hostile attitude, that of a victim bereft of all hope who grabs the first hand of salvation offered with the stiff gestures of a castaway.

We walked up the calle de Santa Isabel in silence, she was still crying and I didn't know what to say, but I felt obliged to keep guiding her with my arm around her shoulders, though the thought of running into Roque terrified me.

When that scene has come to mind since (without my summoning it up), I've noticed that almost immediately I find the memory embarrassing and that Rosario seems cloying, but then I have to recognise that I let it happen, no-one sent me to sit down beside her and put my arm around her shoulders and tell her I was fond of her. It was the first time in my life – and the last – that I stroked a stranger without having erotic intentions. So, what had happened? Was it some sort of homage to Dante?

As I preceded her, this time it was me in the rôle of Virgil, up the steep steps to the garret, asking all the saints in heaven for Roque to have left, I was already conscious that the afflicted being following me was the counterpart of the one who knew exactly how to separate order from chaos in words. The lecturer with the granny glasses had disappeared, leaving as a sequel the ambitious, impatient and slightly resentful provincial type that her later confidences gradually revealed. Much less talented, moreover, at the epic narration of her own woes than at lyrically depicting the irremediable suffering of the entire human race.

Fortunately Roque wasn't there, he'd left me a note saying he'd come by in the evening with the motorbike to see if I felt like going for a ride.

By the time he came to pick me up at 8 p.m., I'd shipped Rosario Tena off to the maisonette, because one of her most urgent problems was finding a place to stay. My head was pounding and I was exhausted. I told him to come up for a minute if he wanted to but that I had a headache and didn't feel like going out.

He came up and, even though I knew how little he liked emotional stories, I sumarised Rosario's for him. She came from a fishing family in Santander, had been a brilliant scholarship student, no longer had a job and had just left the house where she'd been living in Madrid, because relations with her brother-in-law, owner of a bar in Moratalaz, had become intolerable, and her sister wouldn't stand up for her, took her husband's side, it was all rather sordid.

"Not everyone has the same luck," I said to Roque. "Apparently, they laugh at her because she wants to be a painter."

"A painter? But isn't she the one you said gave such great lectures?"

"Yes, she's really good, the best I've had, but she doesn't see it like that, since she was little she's dreamed of being recognised for her own work and plans to give it her all. She's had an exhibition in some towns up north, she says, but nothing more."

"And how's her painting?"

"I don't know. My mother will know more about that. I rang to ask her to take care of Rosario, whom I sent over to the maisonette. She thought I meant to rent it to her but I said no, when she's famous she can pay me rent."

"She must've thought she'd fallen into a fairy tale."

"Probably. Especially when she found out I'm Águeda Luengo's daughter; she couldn't believe it. It seems she's a big fan."

"Why are you looking so miserable then? You've been a fairy godmother, made good use of that maisonette, which causes you such peculiar grief, and you've probably made your mother happy as well."

"If only," I said pensively. "They won't have to see each other much, because the flats are separate. And, anyway, what's mine is mine. But I'd rather they got along."

"That will depend on your mother's propensity to play Pygmalion."

"She never displayed that tendency with me. She's asked me since I was little to prevent her from worrying about my life or trying to influence it, she's scared at the thought of mothers who throw all they've done for their children back in their faces, having convinced themselves that they're owed something that never belonged to them in the first place. She says a life belongs to the person who grabs it and conquers it for themselves. She doesn't protect me, naturally."

Roque was looking at me with the mocking expression of someone with no illusions about this sort of speech. I had never talked to him very much about my mother.

"But honey, what's it got to do with you? You don't figure in all this. People use people of other species for Pygmalion projects, not their own children. These are mysterious things, we can't know what parents feel for such individuals. Maybe getting involved will be her scene. And if it is, I can assure you this offended sister-in-law who dreams of glory is perfect for your mother. Come on now, forget about it, your headache'll blow away with the wind. Let's go, don't bother changing, you're super sexy and there's no time. I've left the bike parked badly outside."

Later, when I went to the first exhibition of paintings Rosario managed to get in Madrid, no doubt through my mother's recommendation, I couldn't help but think of Roque – who by then was giving me more grief than pleasure – and recognise once more the knack he had for pinpointing people, as if they were butterflies in a glass case.

In the first place, Rosario's pictures were pitiful, especially because it would be obvious to any connoisseur that they were despicable and shoddy imitations of my mother's work. But worse than that, she had copied my mother's style of dress and her way of moving and even her voice. My mother's style is too individual for an imitator, especially one so close to her. Rosario moved among Mum's friends in that pink trouser suit, her hair highlighted, attempting a haughty smile, with neither grace nor ease, hanging on her every gesture. At a certain moment, when I went over to say hello, I saw that she understood what I thought of her paintings and about everything else, though I didn't say a word. And then I thought I saw the glint of a raised sword in the depths of her pleasant eyes.

That was when the image of Anne Baxter in *All About Eve* appeared to me for the first time.

XVII

The Devil's Staircase

"It's me, Águeda. Let me in," I said from the street in a firm voice. "You're not asleep, are you?"

And through the intercom I heard a "No! It can't be!" as though from the grave, drowned at the end by a sob that had the hint of a howl to it.

"Come on, don't make a scene," I said impatiently. "Let me come up, please. Or are you with someone and I'm bothering you?"

The only reply was the click of the door, and I pushed it open rather aggressively. I was being too considerate. Rosario's flat was still mine, and now the whole maisonette was too, and all the objects of value it might contain, including the paintings signed by Águeda Luengo, whatever will she had left, or even if she hadn't left one at all, she was divorced from Dad, I'm her only heir. But these mean considerations, so distant from the spur-of-the-moment impulse that had brought me to Bernabeu, were cancelled out by the thought of that signature in the bottom right corner of those sought-after paintings. Sometimes I forget we have the same first name and that we sound quite a bit alike. So my incipient distaste at Rosario's theatrical moan dissolved as soon as I entered the lift and pressed the button for Number 15. Poor woman, it was likely that my "It's Águeda, let me in", so late at night as well, had given her the fright of her life.

That was, in fact, just what had happened. She told me so as soon as she saw me come out of the lift, she was waiting for me with the door open – "Sorry, for a second I thought you were her" – and quickly added that she hadn't dared come to my house, but that she'd started to fear I'd gone away, thank goodness she was going to be able to talk to me before she left, the next day a friend with a van was coming to get her furniture, she wasn't taking anything except her own stuff, not so much as a nail file, there were so many messages she wanted to give me, and the keys, of course, not to mention how much she had to thank me for, she didn't expect to be coming back to Madrid very often for the moment, and all this with her eyes still filled with tears, "at last" and "thank goodness" she faltered several times, even before she'd invited me in, as we stood facing each other on the threshold of the spacious vestibule that leads into my mother's studio, after a compulsive and clumsy embrace that for the moment didn't make things any easier. "You're here, that's what matters, what a relief, thank goodness."

But goodness didn't seem to be holding up too well against evil, or more specifically against the world of shadows, as the lecturer with the granny glasses would have put it, despite all those thank goodnesses that came tumbling out one after another like sneezes. It was hard to imagine that Rosario's face could have worn a grimmer expression before my arrival than the one I saw now. Her whole demeanour called to mind the opacity of the windows of a train abandoned on a dead line. She'd gained quite a bit of weight, she spoke very nervously and she was wearing a blue tracksuit.

I was surprised she'd opened that door and not the one to the flat upstairs, where I'd rung and which has its own entrance, although the lift only reached the two flats on the 15th floor, a separation that had been irreversibly removed in due course by the strokes of a pickaxe. The upstairs flat is much smaller, from the street it looks like a sort of turret.

My mother loved drawing plans, when I was little she used to design imaginary cities for me full of hiding places, later she came to hate hiding places. (I don't mean interior ones; those multiplied, I think, the more walls she knocked down, or dreamt of knocking down.) She'd had that arrangement of open spaces in the maisonette in her head for ages, since not long after Dad had left, and she suggested the idea to an architect friend when she had enough money saved up, that famous maisonette was an *idée fixe*, whenever I saw her consulting a plan or drawing one which she then tried to show me, I ran off saying, "Look, leave me alone, you earn the money, right? So, do what you like with it." She'd always enjoyed interior decorating and she got along well in the company of architects, the more modern the better. Now I'm sorry she didn't get to know Tomás well, and also a little regretful, because that was my fault. Once, when I told him about the maisonette, he said he thought the two independent entrances were a fantastic idea, a great way of accommodating cohabitation, even for couples.

Why had Rosario come down to let me in there? All the lights were on inside and over her shoulder I glimpsed the immensity of those cream and very pale green surfaces, without recesses or any apparent mystery – though who really knew – where Águeda Luengo had feverishly devoted herself to her work for thirteen years, the most important of her career. I hardly ever came here to visit her, that's the truth, but I have the consolation that the last time I did, at the beginning of that same year, was a real celebration and we laughed and laughed.

What we mostly talked about then were partition walls and her mania for knocking them down, "The thing about knocking down walls, my child, just like throwing away junk or papers that only get in the way, is that it's like operating on a tumour, before it turns malignant, or working out at the gym to keep in shape, you know I don't like obstacles between me and the air, you don't understand because you're not old, you young people breathe without noticing." I told her she wasn't old yet either, nor would she ever be, that knocking down walls and throwing away furniture and papers was certainly a mania but not one born of age but rather the opposite, a mania of personality that we all had in some form or other, and I also asked her if she'd said that about going to the gym as a metaphor. "A metaphor? Watch this," and she threw herself down on the floor, and without lifting her bum off the carpet, raised her legs together, perfectly straight and with her toes pointed in an acute angle up to her chest, I tried to imitate her but couldn't. "You'll live to be 100, for sure, Luengo," I told her – when we joke around I call her Luengo – and she said "Oh God no, please." It was an unforgettable evening, just the two of us, who could have believed she had less than a half a year to live. Rosario had gone to Santander for Christmas and Tomás didn't come with me, although we talked a lot about him that evening. "I'm not really interested in becoming friends with his family either, you know? Then things get complicated and we're just fine as we are, though if you want to know the truth . . ." And she interrupted me saying she'd make do with a half-truth, neither of us were brought up to go further than that, serious and smiling at the same time, as if with that confession the responsibility for our errors was divided between the two of us, and suddenly a sweet complicity settled on us, lightening the weight of any confidence. "OK, agreed, well, bearing that in mind, I can tell you I'm pretty uninterested in Tomás's mother, but in my case it's different, I'm the one who doesn't make it easy for you and Tomás to get to know each other better because he'd fall in love with you, I'm sure of it." She started to laugh and said I was hopeless even with an architect by my side, that I'd been born gassy and gassy I'd die, and the mention of bubbles led us to open a bottle of French champagne she had in the fridge, which we drank with a few canapés of caviar and smoked salmon. It had got very late and now it began to snow a little, and through the studio's big windows we could see the lights on the tops of the buildings, dotted with incipient snowflakes that danced in swirls, she was preparing an exhibition called "Urban Geography" and she showed me a few sketches. I said, "You've become a bit of a New Yorker, Luengo," and she shrugged her shoulders with a slightly sad smile. "We become what we can," she said, "it's been a long time since I've measured myself."

I ended up telling her about Vidal y Villalba, who'd been shouting at me from inside my head for more than four years, in order to see if I'd finally get round to dragging him out of those dusty papers and taking serious charge of his story. I'd just recently re-read the first interrogations Don Blas de Hinojosa had conducted in prison, and I spoke quite passionately, spurred on by her expression, seldom had I seen her watching me so excitedly when I was telling her something, or at least as an adult, when I was a little girl she lapped up my stories. "But, Agui, this is absolutely marvellous, it sounds like a thriller, and with the testimony of the servant who pretends to be mad to top it off, you must see you can't leave it half-finished?" "That's exactly what Tomás tells me." She laughed and stroked my hair. "If both of us tell you, you'll drop it for sure, but it'd be a shame." I promised I wouldn't, that I wasn't going to let another year go by before I sat down to write it up, although first I had to put Don Luis's statements and those of his servant in chronological order, as well as the ones from State officials involved with the case and the medical reports, I'd signed up for a computer course, but I didn't always go, I got bored, I just can't get on with those machines. Of course, these were all excuses – I admitted – what was happening was that I was coming down with a known and nameable illness, doctoral thesisitis; and I told her the story of an English lady who'd settled in Simancas, where she spent many years following leads concerning certain people who'd accompanied Columbus on his voyage to America, I think it was, but she never actually wrote anything, she died of old age one morning as she came in to do her research just as she had every day, and there's a plaque in the Archive, marking the spot where she fell as if struck by lightning. And my mother laughed and laughed, in pure peals of good humour, "When you're on a roll, there's no-one I have more fun with."

We barely spoke of Rosario, now I wonder how it was that over the course of all those hours Rosario didn't come up in conversation more than briefly, a mention that she'd been going up to Santander quite often lately, I don't recall noticing my mother avoiding the subject for any particular reason, I probably assumed that Mum's possible Pygmalionism was by that stage focused on a character who no longer interested her. She mentioned that Rosario was turning rather sour.

We stayed up till the early hours in the studio, it was our last memorable conversation and also her last birthday, the night before Epiphany, I'd bought her a scarf made of raw silk.

"You'll come in, won't you?" said Rosario, who was perhaps starting to find my silence strange.

"Look, if you don't mind, I'd rather walk up to the other door," I said pointing to the stairs that led to the upper part of the maisonette. "I'm not really ready to see her studio yet, I hope you'll understand."

"Of course I understand. I feel the same way."

"Then why did you come down to open this door? I rang the bell for upstairs. It's you I've come to see."

"I don't know . . . you're right." She was flustered. "I'll go up and open the door, though it's a real mess, I'm getting all my things together, you're going to get a terrible impression . . ."

"What does it matter, Rosario? I haven't come to pay you a social call," I interrupted her, turning my back on her as I started up the nineteen steps that separated the two levels.

I climbed very slowly, counting them one by one, determined that by the time I reached the top every trace of aggression towards Rosario would be dispelled. The frightened and slightly servile tone of her excuses revealed the anguish of a prisoner cornered by the threat of possible inspection. Well, I wasn't Blas de Hinojosa, nor was I here to interrogate her about what kind of relationship she'd had with my mother, or to settle accounts or drag out dirty linen from the past. This was about the two of us, about our present, about whether we could make peace of a war I was conscious of having started. Living's the strange thing, she was the one who had emphasised that strangeness as the final note of an unforgettable lesson in art and life, a lesson I'd still never thanked her for. Very strange, yes, but we were both still alive, and her brother Miguel and Águeda Luengo were too, as long as we remained able to lift our heads above the chaos and invoke the two of them, and contemplate the brilliance of stars that shine in another hemisphere. That was what I wanted to talk to Rosario about, I'd come to give her back what she'd taught me, to remind her of it so that now it could serve as encouragement for her.

The flat was indeed a disaster area, not just because of the disorderly piles of books and clothes, the open, half-filled suitcases, the paintings – some wrapped, others not – that obstructed every path, but also due to something invisible that only experts could detect: a certain indefinable mix of medicinal smells whose use has always been of little effect against that radical illness located by Fichte in the inertia of the human being capable of putting the merest trace of free will in chains. There wasn't a single seat not covered in junk, and Rosario's sinuous movements as she attempted to create a more pleasant environment failed through their lack of conviction. They were blind lashings-out. I knew all about them. Excluding her own self – I thought, rolling my eyes – there was a certain harmony in that ensemble. A painter would not have been able to arrange objects in such turmoil.

"Do me a favour and keep still," I said. "Don't move anything. If you could see the mess my house is in. Well, since this morning it's a little better because the housekeeper came. Do you remember what Beatrice said to Dante? *You make yourself so dense with wealth / Of false imagination, and cannot see / All that you would if you had freed yourself.* I repeat it to myself like a prayer sometimes, though of course I forget it when I most need to remember it. But that always happens. Things end up finding their place on their own, Rosario, it's a matter of time, leave them, and let yourself float in time, OK? Don't flail against it."

"I shouldn't flail against time?" she asked, pronouncing the words slowly, slightly disconcerted.

"Yes, that's what I said. Come here."

I'd sat down on the carpet with my legs crossed and motioned for her to do the same, as I leaned back against an armchair.

"Come on, come here, what do we need chairs for? I love sitting on the floor, don't you? In that garret in Antón Martín, where you came that one time, I almost never did because of the cockroaches, but I doubt they're a problem here."

Rosario had given up her futile attempts at activity and looked at me, her expression halfway between moved and somnambulant, a bundle of clothes in her arms.

"No. I've never seen one," she said softly. "The worst are the ones on the inside, it's a terrifying infestation. They're the size of buffalos. I'm foundering, Águeda, I swear."

As she pronounced that name her voice trembled.

"Throw all that on the floor and sit down, OK?" I told her with that mixture of authority and gentleness I rarely manage to combine in adequate proportions. "We're not going to cry. We're going to work out our strategy. Remember, to get out of hell the most ingenious way is to take advantage of the steps that, without realising it, the devil himself offers us."

And I smiled to myself as I recalled my "corner pain" of that afternoon, so sharp and recent and nevertheless so distant already. What great advantages I had gained from my encounter with Roque! With the devil, sometimes it's enough to try and remove his disguise.

I was glad to see that Rosario obeyed me without asking questions. She dropped the pile of clothes, sat down in front of me and leaned against the wall, sighed deeply and half-closed her eyes. I let the pause lengthen on purpose. Her face began to emit light. For the first time in a long while I saw the lecturer with the granny glasses. Except that now it was she who seemed to await my instructions.

Instead of giving her any, I crossed the little space between us on all fours and hugged her tight.

"We're not going to founder, you know?" I whispered to her. "We're on our way out. And she's guiding us. Hang on to me."

XVIII

Don Basilio's Farewell

There is a column bearing the date of that night, and it supports the structure of all that came later.

The next morning, despite having slept less than three hours, I felt capable of risky mental acrobatics, and so happy with myself and with the world in general that it must have shown in my face, because Magda noticed it as soon as she saw me sitting on the steps of the Archive, waiting for it to open. She was surprised that I was there so early, but also by how young I looked, seeing me from the distance she'd even doubted it was me – she said, as she scrutinised me carefully as if trying to find a visible cause for the transformation.

"Have you cut your hair?"

"My hair? No."

"Hm, you look different. I don't know what, but something's happened."

"Well, last night I made up with a friend. It was like a deep cleansing."

"Ah, I knew it. After all, the soul and body live on either side of a thin wall, and it's best if they get along like good neighbours." She finished the phrase in a slightly preachy tone.

"Sometimes they're at daggers drawn," I said, "on that you can depend. But where I don't agree is about the wall. I see them in the same room. And of course they go to bed together."

Magda gave me a forced smile. Maybe her religious beliefs

prevented her from accepting that risqué metaphor without hesitating.

"The things you come out with! So," she asked curiously, "were you and your friend really angry with each other?"

"Not angry exactly, it was more of a misunderstanding. But with all sorts of ramifications. I'll tell you about it some time."

"Really? That's great! I spent last night thinking about your husband. In all innocence, you understand," she added, blushing a little. "What I mean to say is I love how you describe things. All that about your drunken binge. It's like something out of a novel."

"Yeah, when we start putting two and two together, each of us has our own novel sealed up inside us. Until you tell someone else, you don't realise it."

"No, you have to have the talent as well," Magda said. "I'm reading a novel right now that, on the surface, is about the experiments of a Victorian entomologist, and a bit about love too, but only a little, it's mainly about the life of insects, and you wouldn't believe it, I'm sorry I've almost finished it because she describes everything well. It's by a woman writer, I can't remember her name, but she's still alive. I tell you, it's one of those books you just can't put down, *Angels and Insects* it's called. You read English, don't you?"

"Yes."

"When I finish it, I'll lend it to you, I bought it last Christmas in London, a friend recommended it."

I didn't let her go on much longer, there were enough novels popping up out of everywhere without having to follow the adventures of an English naturalist who describes the lives of insects. I made a stop sign with my hand. Why don't we leave this for another time?

"When a drawer gets full up to the top, no matter what you do, nothing more fits in, Magda, and suitcases too, not even sitting on top of them helps; and, of course, you're always left with things you don't know what to do with. That's just what happened to my friend and me last night, she's moving to Santander, I'll tell you about it later. And you can tell me about the naturalist, OK?"

"OK," she smiled. "But your story is more intriguing, I can see it in your face."

There was a lot to do that day and I was able to attend to everything with efficiency and in good spirits, although every once in a while my attention wandered off to Rosario's novel, reliving it through the words that had finally burst from her as if from a dark well – thank goodness – like buckets of fresh water. And I had also spoken, it wasn't too difficult to mimic her actions, it was really just a matter of making the effort, and how marvellous it had felt. The pulleys of our respective wells squeaked, we pulled the ropes and drank from those buckets left emptied as soon as they appeared at the rim, we were both thirsty. We had a craving for Águeda Luengo, to see her reflected in each other's eyes.

I began to understand that Mum's death had left Rosario more bereft and isolated than it had me, her orphanhood was that of one who awakens suddenly in the middle of the desert after experiencing a prolonged mirage. I hadn't experienced any mirages. I'd known for a long time that my mother was not one person but several, and although I didn't know them all, I guessed that none would be willing to allow herself to be bled dry by exclusive love; we were cut from the same cloth. But there was also something that no-one could ever take away from me: my privileged childhood. In Rosario's own miserable and inhospitable youth, with no more resources than those of her imagination, she'd gradually fostered, like two allied forces, an ambition for prosperity and the tendency to be dazzled by what she'd never had, what she'd found only in literature.

She had read voraciously, everything that fell into her hands since she was small, influenced by her brother Miguel, who had gone into a seminary and then left it. She named him many times as she spoke, Miguel, may he rest in peace, the only member of the family who encouraged her inclinations, a great poet. What she wanted was to paint, to escape from daily sordidness through colour. She would sit on the dock waiting for her father's boat to return, breathing in the smell of the sea, looking at the sunset through lowered eyelashes, and it was as though she saw a bridge drawn between her own hunched form and unexplored worlds that seemed to call for her, a delicate bridge and perilous too, she knew, but she rebelled against the idea of staying quiet forever within that composition like a grey stain. One day she'd transfer to canvas not just iridescent changes of light but also the opposing sentiments that inspired a fleeting brushstroke of mother-of-pearl crowning the clouds, or the unexpected inkling of a storm.

Her words managed to convey this symbiosis with intense precision, something I'd never seen in her paintings. She painted more with her mouth than with a brush – how was it that she didn't see this? The results were light years apart, and I told her so when any barrier between us had completely disappeared and I was drunk on her story, which wavered between fear and hope, listening as she revealed, as illustrations, a mule boy painted by Giotto, bending down to drink water that San Francisco has brought forth from a rock, and then a sonnet by Juan de Arguijo that she'd known by heart since childhood, "Storm and Calm". It's in *The Thousand Best Poems of the Spanish Language*, and always seemed rather conventional to me, but when she recited it, it created an angry sea behind her, "rising its fury and the storm rises", as a black cloud blinds the glowing red sun. Rosario closed her eyes and leant her head against the wall and her chest heaved, and then began to go quiet with the final lines:

But later I saw the black veil break,
dissolving into water, and the clear day happily
restored to its original brightness,

And gazing on the sky lovely with a new splendour,
I said, "Who knows if a similar change
is not in store for my fortunes?"

And then I couldn't hold back any longer and I told her, "Look, Mum didn't do you any favours by encouraging you to follow in her footsteps – if that's what she did – you don't have to follow in anyone's, the artist appears from the bundle of calamities you are when you start looking at art and literature from the point of view of your anxiety to escape the inferno, that's where you derive your power of metaphor from, you transform what you say into a path of light for others, everyone in class noticed it, they were left speechless, there's never been a lecturer like the one with the granny glasses in that department, I swear to you. Listen to me, take those exams! You were born to teach, and that's all there is to it."

Rosario listened to me, absorbed and pleased, my mother had never suggested that. "Maybe because she didn't know your oratorical gifts. Did you express yourself to her in the same way you do to me?" Rosario shook her head, no, passion dazzles, and the need to be loved and to invite admiration makes us vulgar. And talking about one's own life is also very difficult, you soon realise you're doing nothing but scratching at the surface of one of many layers.

I sensed that we were edging towards a taboo subject: her relationship with my mother.

Once we were in her studio, where we'd finally gone so I could collect some clothes, jewellery and papers of hers, Rosario mentioned how hard Mum was to love, and I confined myself to answering that I knew. But the fog Águeda Luengo hid behind wasn't cleared for me by the testimony of Rosario Tena nor, two days later, that of my grandfather, if those vacillating contributions could be called testimony. Mum remained in profile at a distance like a sphinx in the mist, that's her condition, her *tarannà*. "It does us no good to be obvious," she used to tell me.

Remedios, who'd been coming up morning and afternoon to get the house ready for Tomás's return, put a few little tucks in one of my mother's favourite outfits, one with a blue silk jacket, which she wore a lot in the summer. It was just a tiny adjustment, said Remedios kneeling down, with her sleeve full of pins, just a couple of centimetres to the seams at the waist, the rest fitted perfectly. "Turn around, let's see, do you want it a bit shorter?" "No, no, just there, just below the knee." "The lady wasn't fat, God rest her soul, she must have had a smashing figure, she probably worked out," and I said yes, she went to the gym all the time, and Remedios, who considered herself eagle-eyed, was delighted to have guessed. "I wonder if you could have it done for me tomorrow?" "Don't worry, I'll run it through the machine tonight," and she gave me a cheeky smile. She could tell from a mile away – she said – that I wanted to look good for when my husband came home, right? "But naturally, child," she finished, without waiting for a reply, "you're doing the right thing, it won't all be sadness."

I wasn't thinking about Tomás, but about my grandfather, when I saw myself in that dress and then when, as soon as I got home from work, I opened her jewellery box with little cushioned slots where she kept her brooches, hair clasps and rings. I tried on several of them and experimented with hairstyles like the loose bun that suited her so well. I approached the mirror and felt on the verge of passing the test, what was I waiting for? I said slowly: "The secret of happiness, Papa, lies in not insisting," and it didn't sound bad at all.

Then one evening at 8 p.m., already dressed, my hair up and jewellery on, I strode over to the telephone and realised to my enormous surprise that there already, at the other end of the line, even before I'd dialled any number, was the necessary voice, that voice my imagination associated with a metallic blue.

"Hello . . . This is Ramiro Núñez . . . Señorita Soler?"

"Yes, speaking, but, what a coincidence! I was about to ring you this very second, I was just picking up the phone . . . Pure telepathy, no?"

I was surprised by the confident and relaxed way that I was able to speak to him, it happens when I see myself looking good, I was in front of a mirror. But I soon ignored my image in order to attempt to pin down his, barely sketched in my head, I didn't even know where he was calling from. "He's someone who takes his time before saying things," I reminded myself. But his silence troubled me.

"I was going to phone you because . . . Did you get my letter?"

"Yes, yes, three days ago."

"Well then, you'll know that I have no objection to your plan. If you give me the green light, I'll go and visit my grandfather right now. I don't think it's too late, what do you say?"

"Yes," he answered emphatically. "Come as soon as you can and we'll talk here. I'll wait for you."

The metallic blue had shed its mysterious reflections. I heard the serious voice of a doctor, and nothing else.

"What's going on?" I asked.

"I'll tell you when you get here. Nothing right now. But come. Your grandfather has asked for you. I'll wait for you in the garden. How long will you be?"

"That'll depend on the traffic."

He had, indeed, come out to wait for me and was sitting on a bench in the garden, smoking. Grandfather, after reading my letter, had fallen completely silent and was refusing to eat or take his heart medicine. He refused visits to his room with agitated, hostile gestures but without saying a word. The night before he'd had a minor stroke, which was causing aphasia.

"In other words," I interrupted, "it's no longer that he won't speak but that he can't."

"Exactly."

"How can you tell the one from the other? By the gestures people use?"

"Yes, there are symptomatic gestures, of anxiety, of difficulty; we can recognise them easily. The patient suffers greatly when he realises he can't speak, that his voice won't come out, then all the things he wanted to say pile up in his head and flutter around as if inside an empty glass room. I think it's at moments like these that patients must understand what air circulating through vocal cords means, entering and leaving the lungs without any obstructions."

I breathed deeply and then, responding to him, I was as aware of what I was saying as of the miracle of hearing my own voice.

"That's what happens with all privileges," I said, "we think of them as toys that we can allow ourselves the luxury of doing without, but that's only until they are taken away. And did you say my grandfather's started talking again?"

"He finally spoke, yes. Two hours ago. And the first thing he said was that he wanted to get up and that we should call you."

"Me or her?"

"Well, he said, 'I want Águeda to come.'"

There was a brief silence. The sun was setting, soon the crickets would start to chirp. In the distance, like the first time I came, was the Valle de los Caídos in profile, although not beneath a stormy light this time. The legs of the tall man seated next to me on the bench were not the same either. They were those of the doctor who looked after my grandfather, their proximity heralded no storm. I looked at him.

"That doesn't really clarify things, doctor. My name's Águeda too. Did he say anything else?"

"Lots more, yes. But nothing that made any sense. I'm afraid he's embarked on an irreversible mental breakdown. It might be the sign of another, more serious attack."

I didn't know how to answer. Now I felt afraid at the thought of the visit. I needed some extra energy. And I looked for it in the gaze of Ramiro Núñez, in his serious eyes.

"What do you suggest I do?"

"Go in and see him, of course, but not for very long. I'll come up to get you in half an hour. Let's go."

We stood up, and he took me by the elbow.

"And how should I talk to him? Respond to what he says? I'm scared my letter might have . . ."

"Your letter," he interrupted me, "was the right card to play, we couldn't have waited much longer, you were very brave, Señorita Soler, to throw it on the table. And besides, I was the one who suggested the game. Therefore any pangs of conscience should be mine. For now, let's forget it, because there's nothing to lose. Don Basilio's life is coming to its end, you should face this fact, and do whatever comes from your heart. His is now a ship that's lost its helmsman."

We went into the building, he walked with me up to Room 309, and stopped for an instant before knocking. He looked at me intensely.

"You don't seem like the same person who was here a week ago," he said, "allow me to congratulate you."

I lowered my eyes. "Of course not, I'm disguised as my mother."

"You're mistaken if you think that's what I meant. You haven't disguised yourself as anyone. Just the opposite. I didn't even mean that you're prettier than last time. It's that I find myself with someone who doesn't hide, who goes to the heart of the matter, a real person. And I know your mother would be pleased to see you like this, the way I'm seeing you."

"Thank you for saying so," I said trying hard to control my emotions. "Shall we knock?"

"Yes," he whispered; "if anything happens, there's a bell by the bedside table. I won't be far away."

Ramiro Núñez's right hand rested briefly on my shoulder and I felt his friendly squeeze of encouragement. Then the knuckles of that same hand rapped gently on the door.

"Is it all right to come in, Don Basilio? Águeda's here."

"Come in!" my grandfather said from inside.

Ramiro opened the door and let me pass, without moving from the threshold.

"I'll leave her with you for a little while," he said in a loud voice. "But I don't want you getting tired, understand? See you soon."

He shut the door and I heard his footsteps going down the corridor.

Grandfather was sitting with his back to me in an armchair, propped up among big cushions, and he didn't turn around when I came in. I walked over timidly. He hadn't lost his hair and he still had excellent posture.

He seemed to be talking to himself. When I got close enough to see the hooked profile of his nose beneath his bushy eyebrows, I realised that he was making confused almost imperceptible sounds, and that he showed no interest in acknowledging my presence, despite having given express permission for me to enter. His clear "Come in!" contrasted markedly with that shapeless soup of dactyls and gerunds he was chewing. I stopped as if before an ambush; was he trying to disorient me, to test me? Sometimes my susceptibility makes me mistrust others, I attribute my own deviousness to them, in this case the suspicion was based on kinship, when all was said and done, he was still my grandfather. He was managing, naturally, to make me nervous. And the worst thing, as always when I get nervous, is that I never know what to do with my hands. They were superfluous. And when I told him so, just like that, simply because I couldn't stay quiet any longer, I knew that I was tossing the first coin in the air. And it transformed me into that little girl who'd pulled back a red curtain, snuck into her grandfather's office, and wanted him to know it and pay attention to her, interrupting his thoughts.

"I tell you, I don't know what to do with my hands. Sometimes they're useless appendages. That's why people smoke. How about you, when you sleep, where do you put them, under or on top of the covers?"

It was an excrescence of the purest sort, something that risked nothing, but I noticed that I'd managed to dispel the buzzing that had been coming from his lips. He began to speak, and even though he still hadn't looked at me, it was clear that the person who was leading him to rave was me. In other words ignoring my presence in his room had indeed been a trick. I smiled. Now then, let's see if we can at least have a little fun here. I had no desire to treat him like a dying person. That was too final.

"My hands, day and night, on top of the Parcheesi board," he said, "I take it out and divide up the counters, mix them up, one or two might fall, Alfredo doesn't mind playing with the yellows, he's even more addicted than I am, bad colour, I tell him, who starts, the sound of the dice box and busy hands, I'm reds or blues, Don Claudio used to like the greens, but the yellows, 'get thee behind me!', you'd have to be mad, for you the yellows, Alfredo, seeing as you don't care, although bad luck comes in by yellow, I always warn him, remember Molière, but he says no, superstitions are daft, bad luck can get in anywhere or not at all, just like good luck, he's right there, but I don't tell him so, he hasn't read Molière. So much time lost playing Parcheesi! The sawdust is swept away and our hands evaporate, another six, that one's mine, off you go, I count 20 and take the green of Don Claudio's that was on its way to safety. Nothing's safe, not even Parcheesi, the bites come from there, it eats us up without leaving marks, and what for, just to keep our hands busy . . . and all those articles in the *Espasa* yet to read. We pay dearly for not knowing what to do with our hands. It's a trick, don't play tricks, Alfredo."

I began to follow the invisible bulk of that player, there was no sign of him, but the yellow counters glowed like gold coins in the dark. I felt grandfather was dragging me into a ghostly dance.

"Do you still play Parcheesi with Alfredo?"

He took a while to answer.

"He doesn't come," he said, "I call him at night, when I'm really bored. But he doesn't come. And playing alone is like going over and over the story of the good seed, it doesn't even put me to sleep . . ."

I was still standing, still hadn't passed the line of his armchair. Outside the window, where he was staring, night had begun to fall. We were almost in darkness.

I knelt at his side. I needed to get him to look at me. One of those hands I didn't know what to do with rose, overcoming an obscure resistance, up to the level of the arm of the chair and alighted there like a stray bird that bit by bit begins to find warmth in another's nest.

"Don't go over and over things, Papa," I said sketching a faint caress on his sleeve. "The secret of happiness lies in not insisting."

And then, in reply, a bony hand came to cover mine. It gave no warmth. Nor did his somewhat spectral voice, that finally answered.

"That's what you said when you came back from your honeymoon," he said slowly. "And then look, what happened happened."

I felt I needed to go on the defensive; it was a cunning gambit: and I reacted viscerally. That man was not going to have a go at my father, no way. I knew they'd never got along.

"There's nothing I need to look at!" I said angrily, as I fled from the touch of that cold hand. "Leave Ismael alone. What are you referring to? What happened?"

"Nothing, nothing, don't get riled, you insisted . . . because you'd gone mad, after all your laughing at love!"

"But what did I insist on? Come on, say whatever it is . . . On what?"

"That he should understand you . . . And he didn't understand you . . . he never understood you . . . you can't ask for pears from an elm."

A few stars were shining outside the window now. I stared at them, engrossed. I had a hard time imagining Águeda Luengo overcome by love, begging violently for fruit from that elm, but on the other hand it was a redemptive fantasy, one of those that helps you breathe easier. When I could speak again, my voice had softened.

"Nor I him, Papa," I said slowly, relishing what I was saying. "I never understood him either. It's very difficult to understand other people. Especially when you're in love."

He looked at me through half-closed eyes. I was about to offer him his thick glasses that were resting on top of a volume of the *Espasa*, but I didn't, afraid he'd see in my own features, a face fallen after having smashed a vase on the floor, unbecoming of you, honey, why did I have to mix everything up like this? His silence frightened me. We were walking on treacherous ground.

"So, who told you to go and fall in love again, might I ask?" he said to my surprise.

He was referring to my letter. Roque vanished, but now I had to invent something. I shrugged. I was escaping one labyrinth only to head straight into another.

"No-one tells you to do something like that," I said evasively. "It happens and that's all there is to it."

On top of my tilted head, leaning now on the arm of that worn-out, anonymous chair, I felt Grandfather's hand touch my pinned-up hair slowly. It was a furtive manoeuvre. I held my breath.

"You're wearing your hair differently," he said. "Is this how your new boyfriend likes your hair?"

"I don't know," I answered in a whisper, "we haven't seen each other for a week. He's working out of town."

"Out of town? What does he do?"

"He's an architect."

It was such a relief to be able to talk to my grandfather about Tomás, I was sick of labyrinths.

"An architect? Well, you'd like that."

"Yes, and I like him, too, you know? The way he is, over the years I've started appreciating that more, in Catalan they call it '*tarannà*', character, finding a character that matches mine, the physical side is important too, of course, but it's not the only thing to look for, I used to look more at the body than at the character. You know I'm a hard one to love, I can't stand anyone clingy, but I don't want them indifferent either; and Tomás – his name's Tomás – well, I don't know, I think I've found the man of my dreams. And he encourages me in my work as well."

Grandfather kept quiet. He kept stroking my head, but with more intent now, more knowingly. But what he said next was the last thing I was expecting.

"You should tell her that," he said after a pause. "You say she's detached, that what you do is all the same to her, but you could be wrong, I'm sure she needs you more than we think, nothing should come between you and her . . . that's all I'm saying, first things first. And if not, then you shouldn't have had her."

"Shouldn't have had her? Are you mad?" The words seemed to burst from my soul. "She is the first thing to me! Nothing comes between me and my daughter, nothing and no-one, for your information! My daughter is what I love most in this world . . ."

My voice was veiled with tears.

"Well, tell her," he said, "tell her that too, she's the one who needs to know it, not me, tell her like that, like you told me . . ."

"I'm telling her now!" I said, shouting now, a crazed tone of voice that was beyond my control.

I tried to calm myself, closed my eyes and they stung as if scorched by little snakes of fire. What I wanted most was to scream "Grandpa!" I knew that if I said that word the evil spell would be broken, but it wouldn't come out, I said it in my head, and it exploded into incandescent fragments, Grandpa, Grandpa, Grandpa.

He had stopped caressing me, it was as if he had a malign power over me, what test was he preparing for me now? The cinema again, the unexpected memory of movies like *Gaslight*, and I found it almost irresistible to hear my name, at last, pronounced by him.

"Águeda."

I breathed deeply.

"Yes?"

"Do you remember that train ticket? Do you still have it?"

It seemed to be an important question. A final test. And I couldn't say: "Look, Grandpa, I give up, I didn't study that lesson, you win." I sat up straight, instead, and swallowed.

"You know how little I like to keep old papers," I said, "but of course I remember, it'll be around somewhere."

I glanced over at him and saw that he was smiling. It's difficult to fool a wolf from the same pack. He hadn't fooled me by pretending to be mad either. And when he began to sum up the lesson I'd shown myself ignorant of, I knew he wasn't talking to Águeda Luengo, not now, although he pretended to be.

"That train derailed and was about to go over a cliff, we didn't have a scratch on us, though there were some serious injuries, our carriage on the edge of the abyss, but if it had fallen all the way, then so long, none of us would be here, your mother, seven months pregnant, the first thing she did was grab hold of her belly with both hands – grab hold of you, obviously – and then calm me down, don't look over the edge, Basilio, it's worse if you look, there we were, hanging off the edge the three of us; that day we were all born, one more jolt and it would have been all over, not a trace, you see, none of us would be here, not me, not you, not your daughter, nor the children she might have . . ."

I stood up, I couldn't take any more. I turned on the light, handed Grandfather his glasses and stood in front of him.

"Not my daughter? Let's speak openly, now. What daughter, may I ask? Look at me. What daughter?"

He didn't want to take his glasses, he flailed about like a trapped insect. I started to feel remorse. He covered his eyes with his left arm while with the right he pushed me away like a diabolical image.

"Yours, I said! Your daughter. And that's that. Don't try to make me talk, damn you . . . Turn off the light, I can't, turn it off, turn it off . . ."

I turned off the light immediately, but he didn't calm down. His whole body shook, he grabbed on to the arms of the chair and started burbling confused sounds after that "turn it off", breathing with difficulty, between snorts, until I realised that he wanted to keep talking and couldn't. Another attack. This time for real. And I'd set it off.

I hurried over to the bedside table, felt around for the bell and pressed it several times. Then I went out to the corridor, although he seemed to be motioning me not to.

I didn't close the door. I stayed on the threshold, watching over what happened inside and out. Ramiro Núñez didn't keep us waiting, he quickly appeared at the end of the corridor, accompanied by a nurse. They walked very swiftly, but in measured steps, like robots, bringing various pieces of equipment.

"What happened?"

"I don't know, I think he's worse. It's my fault. I need some air."

"Don't worry. Go down to the garden."

They went in, turned on the light and I saw them pick him up gently by the arms and legs to lie him down. He struggled, put up a fight.

I went to get my bag, and as I was about to leave, I noticed that on the table, beside the *Espasa*, was the letter I'd written to my grandfather the night of the Indian settlement. Around it were three or four balls of crumpled paper, drafts he'd discarded. I took one furtively. They had removed Grandfather's clothes. I saw him from an angle. He looked like a fakir.

"Doctor, I'll wait downstairs. Please don't be too long."

He didn't take long to come down and meet me in the garden. He found me smoking. I'd had time to decipher and memorise Grandfather's message, written in trembling letters and then discarded: "I think I'm going to that country where the post doesn't function very well, too," it said. "I don't know if I'll be able to write to you."

Ramiro Núñez couldn't spend much time with me. He said that Don Basilio was responding and that he could recover from that attack in the same way he'd recovered from the earlier one, that I should go home, he'd keep me informed. He asked if I'd managed to talk about anything coherent.

"It would take a long time to tell," I said. "And I don't know if you could understand it. It was really about family labyrinths. I'll tell you one thing; it may be that it runs aground tonight or in a year's time, but that ship, Doctor, does have a helmsman."

When I got home, Tomás had returned. And he was waiting for me, because as soon as he heard the sound of my key, he opened the door. It seemed the most natural thing in the world, the most deserved, and I clung to him immediately, unable to say anything but his name. But that was already a lot, because it reaffirmed evidence confirmed by touch, smell and his response to my embraces. He didn't say anything either until we separated to look at each other. His expression was serious.

"Your grandfather has died," he said then. "The doctor just rang. That's where you've come from, isn't it?"

We went inside, and I dropped on to the sofa in the living room, I took off my high heels and all the clips holding my hair up in a style that wasn't mine and it fell down my back. My neck hurt. I started to rub it with my fingers. Tomás stood in front of me watching me in surprise, but there was a sensuous glow in his eyes as well.

"I've never seen you look more beautiful, never in my life. Please don't cry," he added, kneeling at my feet. "You didn't have much to do with your grandfather, did you? And besides, I'm here now. Tomorrow I'll go with you to arrange the funeral, I'll help you sort out the paperwork, don't cry, please."

He sat beside me on the sofa, we started kissing.

"Thank goodness you've come home, I was dying to see you, I'm sick of death, sick of inheriting other people's stories, sick of lies, I just want to see you, be myself in your eyes, for your life . . . everyone gets in my way, I can't stand shadows between me and you . . ."

That very night I became pregnant.

Epilogue

I woke up very early today, saw that Tomás and the child were still sleeping and I've come quietly downstairs to make coffee. We live in the maisonette now, but so altered that Mum, if she raised her head, wouldn't recognise it. I'm thinking of this as I contemplate the details of this spacious and bright kitchen-dining room designed by Tomás, waiting to hear the water in the coffee pot begin to bubble. Despite how big this downstairs area seemed to me when it was all one open space, I never imagined that you could get out of it, apart from the kitchen, a large living room, an office, a guest room with a bathroom, several cupboards and a pantry. The bedrooms and Cecilia's playroom are upstairs. My daughter's name is Cecilia. She's one-and-a-half years old.

In three days it will be Christmas Eve, it's Sunday and I've had to turn on the light because the sun's not up yet. A thick fog hides the buildings opposite.

I turn off the gas because the coffee's ready, pour myself a cup and take it on a tray to the little corner of the kitchen where there's a desk. It was Tomás's idea. He wants me to have a handy space, just in case I'm visited by inspiration while cooking or feeding Cecilia, a place where I can lean my books and papers without getting them covered in yogurt.

A week ago I got back to work on the story of Vidal y Villalba and I like to go over things in the mornings. It's like searching my memory. On 14 October 1788, still in prison in Madrid, he declared before Don Blas de Hinojosa that he could not summon sufficient strength of mind to continue his confession "with the steadiness required". As I enjoy this morning's first coffee, I look for Don Blas de Hinojosa's report, in which he doubts the forgetfulness of the prisoner, who accuses himself of being insane:

> . . . but his own absurd and irrelevant replies, writes Hinojosa to Floridablanca, have such connections between them that they must be meditated and planned to persuade of madness, by the prisoner in his right mind. To convince this man to leave off these pretences and enable me to close the case, I've ordered in view of his tenacity that he be placed in two pairs of crossed fetters and manacles, which are the ordinary constraints in such cases. But since his declared aim is to take his own life he has not wanted to hobble from the place in which he was sitting even to relieve himself . . .

I interrupt my reading because I hear the upstairs door open. I stand up and peek around the bottom of the staircase.

Cecilia is coming down very slowly, holding the bars of the banister. She's wearing her pyjamas with blue diamonds, her favourites. She stops and we look at each other.

"Where?" she asks curiously.

I look around for the cat, who's dozing on an old cushion. I assume she means him, because they're very good friends.

"Over there," I tell her, pointing.

Gerundio opens one eye lazily and closes it again. Cecilia doesn't show much interest in his presence either, she says only "cat" in a distracted tone of voice and continues down the steps until she arrives at my side. She raises her hands high as if exploring a phenomenon invisible to me.

"Where?" she repeats.

I lift her up in my arms and we walk over to the big window with our faces together.

"Far away," I tell her, "we can't see because of the fog. Beyond."

She makes a careful, circular gesture with her hand as if she wants to investigate all of it, take it all in.